# DAWNMAN PLANET

Ron Bronston was sworn to protect the United Planets' dream—the pursuit of freedom and progress on all of the 3,000 human-inhabited planets of the galaxy.

As an operative of the secret section of the United Planets' Bureau of Investigation, Bronston was called upon for some very unusual missions. But the present crisis was without precedent.

Man's sovereignty in his galaxy was challenged by a single madman and the super-weapons of the Dawnmen, the mysterious aliens from the unexplored vastness of the galaxy's center. Bronston, alone, had to find a way to stop them.

# *DAWNMAN PLANET*

by

Mack Reynolds

**WILDSIDE PRESS**

# PART ONE

## I

Supervisor Sid Jakes was in fine fettle. As his men inspected the papers of the VIPs at the door and finally ushered them into the highly guarded room, he took over and pleasured himself in presenting the exhibit.

The exhibit was in a square box which resembled a combination coffin and deep freeze, which is exactly what it was. The exhibit itself was a small charred creature about the size of a monkey or rabbit. However, signs of clothing or harness could be made out, and what would seem to be side arms.

The routine went almost identically with each visitor. At the door, Ronny Bronston, or one of the other Section G operatives, would finish the identification and call out such as, "Sidi Hassen, Hereditary Democratic-Dictator of the Free-wealth of the Planet Medina."

The ruler of Medina would come forward, invariably blank of face; and with a gesture, as though presenting his most valued possession, Sid Jakes would indicate the exhibit.

The Section G agents had come to expect the same initial reaction each time.

It was: "What is it?"

Sid Jakes would grin happily, but hold his peace.

The VIP, his eyes probably bugging by now, would

say, in absolute astonishment: "Why, it's an alien life form!"

The sharper ones would sometimes say, that first time: "It's an *intelligent* alien life form!"

Supervisor Jakes let them remain long enough to realize the full significance of the badly burned, deep-frozen carcass; then, invariably stemming a flow of questions, he would usher the VIP to an opposite door, where other Section G operatives took over.

The secret room cleared, they would begin all over again.

"His All Holiness, Innocency the Sixteenth, Presidor of the Holy Theocracy of the Planet Byzantium."

His All Holiness would step forward and gape in turn at the charred body of the tiny creature. "It's an intelligent alien life form! But there *is* no intelligent life in the galaxy, save Created man!"

There was only one break in the routine.

Ronny Bronston had been standing to one side for the nonce, while his two companions guarding the door processed the latest arrival.

One of them began to say, "The Supreme Matriarch Harriet Dos Passos of the Planet . . ."

Ronny snapped "She's a fake!"

The newcomer darted in the direction of the freezer box which contained the alien carcass, yelling. "I've got a right . . .!"

Ronny put out a foot, cold-bloodedly, and she went down, arms and legs going every which way.

"Sorry, lady," he said. "Admission is by invitation only."

"Get her, boys" Sid Jakes snapped, coming forward quickly himself. Ronny and the other two grabbed for the intruder.

But she was made of sterner stuff than they had assumed. She rolled, bounced to her feet and scrambled toward the freezer.

She stared into its interior, eyes bugging as all eyes had bugged that morning. Finally, she turned and faced them, her expression unbelieving, as all expressions had been unbelieving. She turned to face four cold faces, four leveled Model H hand weapons.

Sid Jakes said, "If she makes one move, any move at all, muffle her." He grinned at the intruder. "That was bad luck for you, the fact that you managed to see it, you silly flat. Do you think we'd go to this much security if it wasn't ultra-important? Now, let's have it. You're obviously not Harriet Dos Passos. Who are you, how'd you get here, and who sent you?"

The other snapped, her voice not as yet shaky, "I'm Rita Daniels, from Interplanetary News. That's the corpse of an intelligent alien life form in there. I'm not stupid. There isn't supposed to be other intelligent life in the galaxy. Our viewers have a right to know what's going on here in the Commissariat of Interplanetary Affairs. United Planets is a democratic . . ."

Sid Jakes interrupted, still grinning "You'd be surprised, my stute friend. Now, once again, who sent you?"

"My editor, of course. I demand . . ."

Sid Jakes made a gesture with his head at one of the Section G operatives. "Terry, take her over to Interrogation. Use Scop . . ."

The news-hen bleated protest, which was completely ignored.

". . . to find out the names of every person who might remotely know about this romp of hers. The editor, possibly her husband, if she has one, the editor's wife, secretaries, fellow reporters, absolutely everybody. Then send out men to round up every one of these. In turn, put them on Scop and get the names of everyone they might have mentioned this to."

"How far do we follow it, Sid?" the agent, named Terry asked.

Sid Jakes laughed wryly, as though the question were foolish. "To the ultimate. Even though you wind up with everybody in Interplanetary News in Interrogation. We've got to have everybody who even suspects, or might possibly suspect, the existence of our little friend, here." He made a gesture with a thumb at the alien in its box.

The agent nodded, then asked one last question: "After interrogation, what?"

Sid Jakes said flatly, "Then we'll have to memorywash her. Completely wash out this involved period, no matter how far back you have to go."

The newswoman shrilled. "You can't do that! Under United Planets law, I've got . . ."

Ronny Bronston shook his head at her. "You're not in the hands of United Planets, in the ordinary sense of the word, girl friend. You're in the hands of Section G."

"But you're a section of the Bureau of Investigation, Department of Justice of the Commissariat of Interplanetary Affairs! I have my rights!"

Sid Jakes didn't bother to argue. He said to his other operative, "Get about it, Terry. This is bad. On your way over to Interrogation, if she makes any attempt to break away, muffle her, but tune your gun low. We don't want her out for too long. She probably had no idea of what she was looking for, when she broke in here. Somewhere there was a leak, we've got to find the source of her knowledge that something was coming off. But, above

8

all, we've got to prevent her from spreading what she saw."

Terry said, "Right, Sid. Come along! You heard the Supervisor. One wrong move and you're muffled; and, believe me, it hurts."

Rita Daniel's last protest, as she was marched out the door, was shrilled back over her shoulder. "You . . . can't . . . do . . ."

"Famous last words." Sid Jakes grinned at his two remaining men. "Come on boys, let's finish. There's only a few more to go." He looked at Ronny approvingly. "That was a neat trick. How did you spot her?"

Ronny snorted deprecation. "She was too romantic. She was wearing makeup disguise, trying to resemble the real Matriarch. She'd have been better off altering the Tri-Di identification portrait in the credentials. We have no record of what the real Dos Passos looks like. She just recently came to office."

They processed the remaining VIPs, then sealed the secret room and put it under armed guard.

Sid Jakes and Ronny Bronston, one of his favorite field men, went on to the conference hall, where they had been sending the viewers of the exhibition.

"Where's the Chief?" Ronny asked. He was what could only be described as a very average man. It was one of his prime attributes as a Section G operative. He was of average height and weight. His face was pleasant enough, though hardly handsome—a somewhat colorless young man of about thirty. He was less than natty in dress and his hair had a slightly undisciplined trend. He had dark hair and brown eyes, and he absolutely never stood out in a crowd.

He was also as devoted an agent as was to be found in

Section G, whose personnel was selected on the basis of devotion to the United Planets dream.

Sid Jakes, walking along beside him—bouncing along, might be the better term—couldn't have been more different. Even his clothes breathed a happy-go-lucky air. He had a nervous vitality about him that made all others seem lazy of movement. But his appearance was as belying as that of Ronny Bronston; one does not achieve to the rank of supervisor in Section G without abilities far and beyond usual.

Sid said, grunting amusement, "The old man's in hiding until the time comes for the big revelation. He's not about to get into that hive of big shots and let them yell at him at random. I'll have Irene give him the word when all's ready."

The selected men of importance of United Planets had been gathered in an Octagon ultra-security conference room, which had been adjusted to hold the full two thousand of them. Comfortable seating arrangements and refreshment, both food and drink, had been provided. However, there was absolutely no method by which any, no matter of what importance, could communicate with the outside.

The doors were guarded by empty-faced Section G agents, under most strict orders. Polite they were, when this president or that dictator, this scientific genius, or that head of a fanatic religious system, demanded exit or some manner of communicating with family or staff. Polite they were, but unbending. When a burly bully-boy, from the feudalistic planet Goshen, tried to be physical, a short scuffle was sufficient to demonstrate that Section G training included hand-to-hand combat.

Irene Kasansky was seated, efficient as ever, at a desk near the podium. She was answering questions, briskly

10

issuing commands into her order box, when requests involved preferred refreshment or other minor matters, which didn't interfere with the security of the meeting.

*There comes a time,* Ronny Bronston thought all over again, *when automation falls flat and man returns to human labor.* In this case, the ultra-efficient office secretary-receptionist. For spinster, Irene Kasansky might be, on the verge of middle age she might be, and unfortunately plain—but she was also by far the best secretary in the Octagon.

Now she snarled from the side of her mouth. "It's about time you got here. I've been through more jetsam, these past few hours, than I've had in the past few years managing Ross Metaxa's office. And I thought that was the ultimate. Where have you been, playing dice?"

Sid grinned down at her. "Don't be bitter, dear. You'll get wrinkles and an acid-looking face, and then everyone will stop propositioning you. All's ready to go. Pry the old man away from that bottle of Denebian tequila and let's let loose the dogs of war."

He turned and bounded to the speaker's stand. Holding up his hands, he called: "Gentlemen, gentlemen, ladies. Can we all be seated? The meeting is about to commence."

He held silence then, until all was quiet, which took some time, considering the fact that the most highly individualistic persons in United Planets were gathered before him.

Sid Jakes grinned finally, as though finding the whole thing amusing, and said, "Undoubtedly, you have been spending the better part of the morning discussing among yourselves the significance of the little creature I displayed to you. But now we shall hear from Commissioner Ross Metaxa."

"Who in the name of the Holy Ultimate is Ross Metaxa?" someone rumbled.

And someone else snapped, indignantly, "You have taken *His* name in vain!" The latter worthy was dressed in colorful and flowing robes.

"Please, gentlemen, please," Sid shouted above again rising voices. "Commissioner Ross Metaxa!" he jumped down from the dais and grinned at Ronny.

"The old man can have this job," he chortled. "Every crackpot genius in this section of the galaxy is out there."

Ross Metaxa came in through an inconspicuous door in the rear of the room, immediately behind the speaker's stand. Eyebrows went up. He was flanked by the Director of the Commissariat of Interplanetary Affairs—as high an officer as United Planets provided; and by the President of United Planets—a largely honorary office chosen by interplanetary vote. Once every ten years, each member planet was entitled to one voice, in selecting the president. Metaxa did not seem to be awed by his companions, but rather was obviously accompanied by peers.

Sid chuckled from the side of his mouth. "The old man's hanging it on heavy."

"He knows what he's doing," Ronny whispered back. "He's going to have hard enough a time as it is, getting this assembly to listen to his opinions."

The Director and the President took chairs off to one side, and Metaxa made his way to the podium. He was a man in his middle years, sour of expression, weighty around the waist, and sloppily clothed to the point where it would seem an affectation.

The voices of the two thousand had begun to rise again, questioning, querulous.

Ross Metaxa glowered out at them for a long moment.

Finally he growled, "All right, damn it, let's cut out all this jetsam and get down to matters."

There was an immediate hush of shocked surprise.

Before an indignant hum could rise again, the Commissioner of Section G announced brusquely: "Ladies and gentlemen, to use an idiomatic term of yesteryear, the human race is in the clutch."

# II

Someone in the first row of the audience snorted ridicule and called up, "Because of that little creature in there? Don't be a flat!"

The Commissioner of Section G looked at him bleakly. "It should occur, even to the physically conscious Grand Duke of the Planet Romanoff, that the size of the creature in question has nothing to do with it." He tapped his head significantly. "It is what is in here that brought us up short. You see, the little fellow was picked up by one of our Space Forces scouts well over a century ago."

"A century!" one of his listeners bleated. "And we are only informed today?"

A buzz began again, but Metaxa held up a wary hand. "Please. That is one of the things I am here to explain. Our little alien was found in what could have only been a one-man fighter scout. He was dead, his craft blasted and torn, obviously from some weapon's fire. His own vessel was highly equipped with what could only have been weapons: most so damaged, our engineers have yet to figure them out. To the extent they have been able to reconstruct them, they've been flabbergasted.

"The conclusion is obvious. Our intelligent alien, in there, was killed in an interplanetary conflict. How long he had been drifting in space, our technicians couldn't determine, possibly only for months, but possibly for any number of centuries. But the important thing is that there was at least one other warlike, aggressive life form in the galaxy, besides man. Probably, at least two, since it was interplanetary war, which killed our specimen."

The buzz rose again, and was not to be silenced for a time. Ross Metaxa stood and waited it out. But they were anxious for his revelations and finally silence ruled.

He dropped another bomb.

"But we no longer need fear our friend in the other room. Man is in no danger from him and his species."

That set them off once more, but he held firm in silence until they quit their shouting of questions, their inter-audience squabblings, chattering and debate.

At last he held up a hand, and said, "Let me leave that statement for a time. Let me lay a foundation upon which to base what we must discuss today."

He looked out at them, thoughtfully. "Most of you are going to have some reservations about what I have to say.

"Fellow citizens of United Planets: When man first began to erupt into the stars, but a few centuries ago, his travels assumed a form that few could have foreseen. All but lemming-like, he streamed from the planet of his origin. And the form his colonizing took, soon lost all scheme of planning, all discipline. The fact was that any group that could float the wherewithal to buy or rent a space transport, or convert a freighter, could take off into the stars to found their own version of Utopia.

"And take off they did, without rhyme or reason. No, I recall that statement. Reasons they had aplenty: Racial reasons, religious reasons, political reasons, idealistic reasons, romantic reasons, socio-economic reasons, altruistic reasons and mercenary reasons. In a way, I suppose we duplicated, a hundredfold, the motivations the Europeans found to colonize the New World. The Spanish came with sword and harquebus in search of gold, ready

15

to slaughter all who stood before them. The Pilgrims came to seek a new land, where they could practice a somewhat stilted religion, in a manner denied them at home. Large numbers of criminals came, either as convicts being exiled or fugitives from justice. Adventurers of every type zeroed-in, seeking their fortunes. Later, large numbers of Germans came, fleeing political persecution, and large numbers of Irish, fleeing famine."

Ross Metaxa grunted, and flicked his heavy head. "And so it was in space. And in the early years, in particular, there was comparatively little friction. The galaxy is immense, and thus far, we have but touched a slightest segment of it. We are way out in a sparsely populated spiral arm, but there are still inhabitable planets in vast multitude and room for all. Every spacer-load of idealists or crackpots could safely find their habitable planet and settle down to go to hell in their own way."

There was a mumble of discontent over the manner in which he was expressing himself, but he went on, ignoring the objections.

"However, in time, some of our more aggressive planets began to have growing pains. Planets, settled by such groups as the Amish, began to worry about their neighbors on the Planet Füehrerland. This had been settled by a disgruntled group of followers of a political leader of the 20th Century, who had come to disaster in his own time, but whose tradition came down through the years, somewhat distorted in his favor, as traditions are apt to become. Suffice to say that United Planets, based here on Mother Earth, came into being. Its purpose, of course, was obvious. To assist man in his explosion into the stars. The very basis of the organization was Articles One and Two of the United Planets Charter. Citizeness Kasansky, please."

16

Irene Kasansky, without looking up, read into her desk mike. "Article One: *The United Planets organization shall take no steps to interfere with the internal political, socio-economic, or religious institutions of its member planets.* Article Two: *No member planet of United Planets shall interfere with the internal political, socio-economic or religious institutions of any other member planet.*"

Ronny Bronston knew, even as she read, that not only Irene, but everyone present in the hall knew the articles by heart. Metaxa was simply using this bit of business to emphasize his fling.

When she was done, Metaxa nodded ponderously. "Over the centuries, most planets, though not all, have joined up. Whatever their stated reasons, usually very highflown ones, the actuality is that each wishes the protection of the Charter. Each planet desperately holds on to its own sovereignty."

There was a buzz again, and again he ignored it.

"Always remember, that within our almost three-thousand member planets are represented just about every political and every socio-economic system ever dreamed up by philosophers and economists since Plato, and every religion since the White Goddess, the Triple Goddess, prevailed throughout the Mediterranean. A planet whose economy is based on chattle slavery doesn't want to have its institutions subverted by adherents of feudalism. And a planet with feudalistic institutions doesn't want some entrepreneur from another planet, flying the flag of free enterprise, to come along with creeping capitalism. An atheistic planet, such as Ingersol, doesn't want a bevy of fanatical missionaries from Byzantium, working away at its youth, which hasn't been exposed to religion for centuries."

His All Holiness of the Holy Theocracy of the Planet Bysantium called out in a fine rage. "I protest your levity, Commissioner."

Ross Metaxa ignored him.

"All this is not new to you. But, somewhat over a century ago, matters changed, overnight and drastically. Our Spaces Forces brought in our little alien, there in the next room. Suddenly we had to face it. Man is not alone in the galaxy. Thus far, we had thought to be. Nowhere, in our explorations, though, admittedly, they have been but a pinprick on the chart of the Milky Way, did we find signs of intelligent life. Lower life forms, yes, occasionally. But never intelligent life of, say, even the order of the chimpanzee of Earth. But now we had to face the fact that there is intelligent, aggressive, scientifically and militarily advanced life in our galaxy; and, obviously sooner or later, man, in his expansion into the stars, will come up against it. It was but a matter of time."

Someone called out. "Perhaps this life form is benevolent!"

Ross nodded his shaggy head. "Perhaps it is," he answered simply.

His words brought a deep silence. These were not stupid men and women. Largely, they were the cream of the planets they represented. The inference was obvious.

Ross Metaxa dropped another bomb. "So it was," he went on, "that the nature of United Planets changed. Unbeknownst to the individual member planets, a new purpose for its being evolved."

There was heavy electricity in the air.

"No longer was it practical for man to allow such groups as the naturalists—who colonized the planet, Mother—to settle into their desired Stone Age society, rejecting all of man's scientific advance down through the ages. No longer could we condone the presence among our number of the Planet Kropotkin, based on the anarchist ethic that no man is capable nor has the right to judge another. No longer were planets such as Monet to be borne."

"Monet?" someone shouted in query.

Ross Metaxa said, "Originally colonized by a group of artists, musicians, painters and sculptors, who had visions of starting a new race devoted entirely to the arts. They were so impractical that they crashed their ship, lost communication with the rest of the race, and, when rediscovered, had slipped into a military theocracy something like the Aztecs of Mexico. Their religion was based on that of ancient Phoenecia, including child sacrifice to the god, Moloch. Monet, too, claimed the benefits of Articles One and Two, wishing no interference with their institutions."

The representative from Goshen, the bully-boy, who had had the run in with the Section G guards earlier, lumbered to his feet. His voice was dangerous. "And what was this new policy adopted by United Planets, unbeknown, as you say, to the member planets themselves?"

The Commissioner made a gesture with a heavy paw. "Is it not obvious, Your Excellency? It became the task of United Planets, though but a fraction of us have been privy to the fact, to advance the human race, scientifically, industrially, culturally, socio-economically, as fast as it was possible to do so."

"*Even though Articles One and Two, the very basis of the Charter were violated?*"

The shaggy head lowered, and Ross Metaxa glowered out at them, in their shocked silence. "No matter *what* was being violated," he growled.

A roar went through the hall and he waited it out.

At long last he was able to say, "Nothing could be allowed to stand in the way of the most rapid advance of which we were capable. Sooner or later, we knew, we would come in contact with the potential enemy. A potential friend, too, of course, but that must remain to be seen. Man must be as strong as possible, when the confrontation takes place."

Sidi Hassen of the Planet Medina was standing. All eyes went to him. Medina was one of the strongest planets in the union, though its government was one of the most repressive.

He said, "Commissioner Metaxa, it is obvious that all this is but a build-up. You have admitted that Mother Earth, home of United Planets, has been secretly subverting the institutions of the member planets. Now tell us why it has been necessary to reveal the fact to us, at this late date." There was a dangerous element in his voice.

Sid Jakes chuckled under his breath and whispered to Ronny Bronston, standing beside him. "Our friend has probably just realized where some of his Underground troubles originated. If the boys have been briefing me correctly, that Hereditary Democratic-Dictatorship of his isn't going to last the week out."

The head of Section G nodded agreement. "Very well," he said. "As I mentioned earlier, the charred body you were all invited to see no longer indicates a threat to us." He paused, wanting the drama.

"*Why not!*" came from a hundred voices.

"Because, a few weeks ago, a small exploration task force, driving out beyond the point thus far ventured to, by even the most adventurous of our race, came upon

20

the three star systems which were the origin of our little dead space traveler."

"You mean," the burly representative from Goshen roared, "that we now know where the sneaky little rats come from and they only dominate three star systems?"

Metaxa nodded. "From all we can find, they had evidently spread over a complex of some twelve planets. Planets similar in nature to those that will support our own life form. Our little aliens were also oxygen breathers." He grunted and flicked his head in his dour, characteristic mannerism. "I see most of you have noted my use of the past tense."

He dropped his last bomb. "Our exploring fleet found that each of their twelve planets were now supporting a methane-hydrogen-ammonia atmosphere. They found also that evidently the switch in atmospheres, from one predominately nitrogen-oxygen, had come so suddenly that the inhabitants had no time to attempt protection. They died. Perhaps some survived for a time, including those that might have been in space, when the atmosphere was switched. If so, it would seem they were destroyed by other means. Perhaps our specimen in the other room was one of these. At any rate, ladies and gentlemen of the human race, this whole life form has been completely destroyed by some other intelligent alien life form beyond it." He looked about the large hall with its some two thousands rulers of the member planets. "That, by the way, should be at least a partial answer to the question of whether or not this life form, still further beyond, can be considered benevolent."

There were a hundred questions being roared at him. He ignored them, largely, trying to answer a few that seemed more pertinent.

Someone called, "Where was this discovery of the three star systems made?"

Metaxa said, "Surprisingly near our member planet of Phrygia, which, of course, is the furtherest from Mother Earth in the direction of the galaxy's center."

Irene Kasansky turned to Sid Jakes and said, "Terry wants to talk to you." She handed him a Section G hand communicator.

Sid spoke into it, his eyes darting around the crowded conference room even as he spoke.

He snapped, "All right, 'I'll be right over." He handed the communicator back to Irene, and said to Ronny Bronston, "Come on, Ronny. They're going to be yelling back and forth in here for hours."

Out in the corridor, Ronny said, "What's up?"

The Supervisor summoned a three wheeler. "Terry's cracked that news-hen Daniels, or whatever her name is. Metaxa doesn't need us for awhile. Let's see what she has to say. Imagine that mopsy's gall, trying to crack Section G security."

They climbed onto the three wheeler, and Sid Jakes dialed Interrogation.

Ronny said mildly, "If you ask me, the woman's pretty stute to have got as far as she did. We ought to recruit her."

"Sure, sure," Sid Jakes laughed. "She'd stay with us for a year or so, until she knew every secret in the Commissariat, then go running back to Interplanetary News again. Once a newshound, always . . . Oops, here we are."

Interrogation had come a long way since the days of the Gestapo of the Third Reich, or even the cellar room

22

with the bright light and the rubber hoses of the Land of Liberty.

Rita Daniels was sitting at her ease in a comfortable chair. Terry Harper was across from her. There was a low table with refreshments between them. Inconspicuously in the background was a Section G stenographer, in case human witness were necessary.

Terry got up when his supervisor entered. He was an old-timer in the bureau, due soon for retirement, which he didn't look forward to. Section G operatives were strong on the dream.

He said, "Sid, as far as the girl knows, only her editor is aware she's here."

While Ronny Bronston sank into the chair, Sid Jakes perched on the stenographer's desk. He said pleasantly to the newswoman, "And how did he find out something was cooking at the Commissariat of Interplanetary Affairs?"

The other's face worked under the pressure of trying to fight off the influence of the drug. "I don't know," she said.

Sid looked at Terry. "You sent a man over to the editor yet?"

"Not yet, Sid. Since, so far as she knows, only the editor is involved, I thought you might want to play it as stute as possible. If we don't have to throw weight around, well and good."

Sid patted him on the arm, happily. "Good man, Terry." He spun on Ronny. "Get over to Interplanetary News . . ." He looked at Rita Daniels. "What's this editor's name?"

"Rosen. He's on the Octagon desk."

Sid's eyes darted back to Ronny. "Bring him over, but in such a way that no ripples are started in his office."

"Oh, great," Ronny said. "No ripples. Just sugar talk him into coming into our lair, eh?"

Sid Jakes grinned at him happily. "Ronny, old boy, if you can't do it ripplelessly, nobody can. You're the most inconspicuous man in the bureau."

"Is that supposed to be a compliment?"

## III

The Nadirscraper, which housed Interplanetary News, delved a good two hundred levels beneath the surface of Greater Washington. As was the prevailing trend, the face presented to the world of the open air was Antiquity Revival: in this case, Egyptian. Although Ronny Bronston had never been in the establishment before, he had passed it on many occasions, never failing to wince at the architect's conception of the Temple of Luxor.

Now he made his way up an immense approach, flanked by a score of marble sphinxes, through an entrada of soaring columns, seemingly open to the sky, but undoubtedly roofed with ultra-transparent plasti.

There was no point in being less than direct. He marched up to the reception desk, pressed an activating button before one of the live screens, and said, "Bronston of the Department of Justice, Bureau of Investigation, to see Citizen Rosen of the Octagon Desk. Soonest."

The voice said, "Your identification, please."

Ronny Bronston brought forth a flat wallet and performed an operation, which came down—unbeknownst to him—in all identicalness, from a long past period of law enforcement.

He flashed his buzzer.

It was a simple enough silver badge, which glowed somewhat strangely when his hand came in touch with it. It read, merely, *Ronald Bronston, Section G, Bureau of Investigation, United Planets.*

"Than kue, Citizen Bronston. Please state your reason

for desiring an appointment with Citizen Rosen."

Ronny said testily, "Bureau of Investigation matter, of a security nature."

"Than kue . . ." the voice faded away.

Almost immediately, a three wheeler approached, and its voicebox said, "Citizen Bronston. Please be seated."

He mounted the scooter, and noted how quickly the pseudo-Egyptian decor melted away, as soon as they had entered a ramp leading into the depths.

The three wheeler took him, first, to a bank of elevators, plunged him an unknown number of levels, emerged, and then darted into corridor traffic.

*Interplanetary News*, Ronny considered. An octopus, which had spread over almost all the United Planets, and over many man-occupied worlds not affiliated with the confederation. Few, indeed, were the planets that could refrain from the fabulous news dispensing service. Even those worlds, such as Goshen, which were so tightly dominated by the feudalistic clique which suppressed it (keeping the populous ninety-five percent illiterate and taking all measures to keep even the barest knowledge of what transpired on other planets from its people), subscribed. In that case, only the nobility had access to the information purveyed.

It reminded Ronny, as he thought, that some measures were going to have to be taken by Section G to overthrow that Goshen aristocracy. If the planet was ever going to get anywhere, the people were going to have to be given a shove out of the mire of class-divided society.

He wondered, vaguely: *how many languages, besides Earth Basic, did Interplanetary News have to deal with? A thousand? Probably, if dialects were considered.* It seemed that a considerable number of the colonists, who wandered off into space—seeking their Ultima Thule—

26

made effort to devise a new tongue, or, at least, to revive a dead one. There must be a score of versions of Esperanto alone, out there in the stars, not to speak of such jerry-rigged artificial tongues as: Ido, Volapük, Lingua Internaciona, Lingvo Kosmopolita, Esperantido, Nov-Esperanto, Latinesce, Nov-Latin, Europan, and what not.

The more closely a world identified with United Planets, of course, the more widespread the use of Earth Basic. But the worlds which attempted to keep aloof, usually for religious or socio-economic reasons, could get so far removed, that United Planets—as well as Interplanetary News—had to deal heavily through interpreters.

There even came to mind that far-out world settled by deaf-mutes. *What was its name? Keller, or something.*

The three wheeler came to a halt before a door.

"Citizen Rosen," its voicebox said.

Ronny dismounted and the vehicle darted off into the corridor traffic.

He stood before the door's screen, and said, "Bronston, to see Citizen Rosen."

The door opened; he stepped through, and into the arms of two well-muscled goons. They held him by his arms, pausing a moment, as though waiting for his reaction.

Ronny mentally shrugged. *It was their ball. Let them bounce it.*

Both, still holding his arms, with one hand, each ran their other hands over him in the classic frisk. He didn't resist.

One leered as he touched under the Section G agent's left arm. "Ah, packing a shooter."

The other said, "Take it, Jed."

Ronny said mildly, "If you take that gun, without my deactivating it first, you're a dead man, friend."

27

The other's hand, which had been darting under his jacket, came to a quick pause.

Jed scowled, "Don't give me that jetsam. What d'ya mean?"

Ronny said reasonably, "It's a Model H, built especially for the Bureau of Investigation. It's tuned to me. Unless I, personally, deactivate it, anyone who takes it from me is crisp within seconds."

The two of them froze.

Ronny said mildly, "If it's as important as all that, suppose I deactivate it for you? And you can return it, when I leave. I'm not here to hurt anybody."

"The boss said . . ."

"The boss is obviously a flat," Ronny said, still with an air of bored reasonableness. "Since when does the Bureau of Investigation send pistoleros around to deal with half-baked newsmen?"

One looked at the other. "The boss said . . ." he let the sentence dribble away.

The other said, his voice gruff, "Okay, give us the gun." Their hands dropped away.

Ronny took the gun from its quickdraw holster, touched a hidden stud and presented it, butt first. "Now, can I see this romantic cloddy, Rosen?"

Jed, at least, flushed; but, one leading, one bringing up the rear, they passed through another door and into a quarter acre of office.

Rosen sat behind a desk much too large for him. He bent a sly eye on the Section G agent.

"So . . . The Department of Dirty Tricks, Section Cloak and Dagger."

Jed put the gun on the desk. "He had this on him," he said; the implication being that they had wrested it away from Ronny in desperate fray.

Ronny said, "Look, you characters seem to have been taking in a lot of Tri-Di crime tapes, or some such. Why don't we cut out all this maize and get around to the reason for my coming over here. We could have simply summoned you, you know."

Rosen said nastily, "You could have summoned till Mercury turned to ice cubes. What's going on over there at the Octagon? What happened to . . ." He cut himself short.

"To Rita Daniels?" Ronny provided. "She's okay. My supervisor asked me to come over and bring you around to discuss Rita and her assignment."

"Yeah? And then you'd have both of us, eh? Listen, Bronston, what's going on? Half the most important bigwigs in the system have . . ."

Ronny said quickly, "I don't believe you really want to discuss this in front of the boys, here."

"Why not?"

"That's what my supervisor wants to talk to you about," Ronny said mildly.

The other stared at him. He was a smaller man, even, than the Section G operative, and there was a cast of perpetual disbelief in his eyes.

He said finally to his two goons, "Go over there to the far side of the room, but keep your eye on this fella. And don't let his size throw you off."

They went to the room's far end and leaned against the wall, assuming expressions of bored cynicism in the best of Tri-Di crime show tradition. Ronny wondered vaguely if it had always been thus, down through the centuries. Did the bully boys and criminal toughs of Shakespeare's day pick up their terminology and mannerisms from watching the villains in plays and aping them? He was inwardly amused.

As yet, Rosen hadn't asked him to be seated. However, Ron pulled up a chair across the desk from the other, his back to the two goons. He looked at the newsman.

"My supervisor wants to talk to you."

"Before he releases Rita, eh?"

There was a certain quality about the other's voice. Ronny assumed the room was bugged.

"I didn't say anything like that," he said, ever mildly. "Where did you get the idea we were holding Rita Daniels?"

"She hasn't returned."

Ronny shrugged. "Why couldn't she be out having a guzzle or two?" He brought a pen from an inner pocket. "Let me have a piece of paper, will you?"

Scowling puzzlement, Rosen pushed a pad over. He failed to notice that the agent—never departing from the standard motions a man makes when he is about to jot down an item—had depressed a small stud on the supposed writing instrument's side. He failed to notice the faintest of hisses, nor the almost microscopic-sized dart that issued from the pen and pricked into his hand.

Even as Ronny scribbled a note on the paper, Rosen, still scowling, absently scratched the back of that hand.

Ronny pushed the note over. It said, merely, *Come along with me, Citizen Rosen.*

Rosen read it and flushed anger. "Do you think I'm drivel-happy?" he began. Then his face went infinitesimally lax, his eyes, slightly strange. Deep in their depths, there seemed to be a trapped fear.

Ronny came to his feet. "Let's go," he said. "Citizen Jakes is waiting."

"Yes. Yes, of course," Rosen said emptily. He stood up also.

His guards reacted.

Jed blurted, "You ain't going with this funker, are you, Boss? You said you expected him to pull some kinda quick one."

Ronny picked up his gun from the desk, reactivated it and slid it back into its holster. He picked up the note he had written and slipped it into his side pocket. Without looking again at the musclemen, he headed for the door, followed by the chief of the Interplanetary News Octagon desk.

Back at the offices of Section G, in the Bureau of Investigation branch offices, still leading, Ronny pushed his way through to the office of Sid Jakes. The irrepressible Sid was sitting at his desk, legs elevated, feet messing up a half dozen reports that lay there.

The supervisor waved a hand in greeting. "Who's this fella?" he asked happily.

Ronny growled, "You wanted Rosen. So here's Rosen."

Jakes peered at the small newsman. "What's wrong with him?"

"He's got a Come-Along shot in him."

"Holy Ultimate, Ronny. You know that's illegal. Interplanetary News will have you on a kidnap romp charge."

Ronny grunted. "Remember? You were going to give this cloddy and his girl, Rita, a memorywash. That isn't exactly part and parcel of the United Planets Charter, either. But one will wash out the recall of the other, so what's the difference? What's going on between all the bigwigs?"

Before answering, Sid Jakes flicked on his order box, and said into it, "Irene, send me an antidote syrette for a Come-Along. Our boy, Ronny, has been tearing up the peapatch. Okay, okay, I know you're busy." He leered. "But who else could I trust with Ronny's neck at stake?"

He flicked the box off, and turned back to his field man. "That old mopsy's sugar on you, you know."

"How's the chief doing?"

"The old man's still at them, hot and heavy. He's let them know the fat's in the fire now. That, willy-nilly, they're going to have to get together in an all-out cooperation, through United Planets, to meet the danger of these new aliens. It's a madhouse."

Sid looked at Rosen. "Sit down, fella. You look tired."

The terror was in the depths of the other's eyes. The wild desire to escape.

Ronny said, "He's tuned to me, of course." He said to the newsman. "Sit down, Rosen."

Rosen sat down.

Sid Jakes flicked his order box again. "Send Terry Harper over with a charge of Scop."

Ronny said wryly, "Our friend here is going to look like a pincushion before we're through with him, what with Come-Along and its antidote, Scop, and then the memorywash."

There was fear and hate in the depths of the eyes again.

Later, shots administered, they sat around, Jakes, Bronston and Harper, and stared at the Interplanetary News man, freed of the kidnapping drug now, but loaded with Scop.

Sid Jakes grinned at him, as though forgivingly. "Now, my stute friend, how many others, besides you and this Rita Daniels, knew about her assignment to break in on the UP conference?"

The other was trying to fight and couldn't. He tried to hold back each word, and couldn't.

"Nobody . . . except . . . my informant."

Sid nodded encouragement. "All right. And who told you about the meeting at all?"

"Baron Wyler."

Sid looked at Ronny and Terry. "Who's Wyler?"

Rosen took it as a question directed at him. "Baron Wyler, Supreme Commandant of the Planet Phrygia."

"Phrygia!" Ronny blurted. "That's the planet nearest to the alien threat. The Space Forces expedition that found the three star systems, where the little aliens came from, took off from Phrygia as its final base."

Sid Jakes chuckled. "Now we're getting somewhere." He bent a cheerful eye on his victim. "And why did the good Baron tell you about the meeting?"

"I . . . I'm not . . . sure. I think . . . it's because . . . he gives us .  . news beats . . . available to him . . . as result . . . of his high :  . . . office. We .  . support . . . his politics . . . on Phrygia." There were blisters of cold sweat on the little man's forehead and his shirt was soaked, but his efforts were valueless. There was hate rather than fear in his eyes now.

"I see," Jakes drawled. "Which would come under the head of interfering with the internal political system of a member planet of United Planets, eh? Naughty, naughty, Rosen. Violation of Article Two. Interplanetary News could lose its license to operate on an interplanetary basis. My, wouldn't your competitor, All-Planet Press just love that?"

But in spite of the levity of his words, his eyes were bleak and he spun to his order box. "If that yoke, Baron Wyler, would break ultra-security to tip off a newsman, who knows who else he might sound off to?" He flicked a switch, and blatted, "Irene, have the boys pick up Baron Wyler of the planet Phrygia and bring him here. Absolutely soonest. Kid gloves, he's a chief of state."

The order box squawked a reply and Sid Jakes winced. "All right. Find out soonest where he's staying and send the boys to get him."

He turned to Bronston and Harper. "It's the most delicate situation that's come up in the history of the UP. We've got almost three thousand member planets, but the leaders of only two thousand were let in on the crisis. If the word gets out to some of these more backward, reactionary or crackpot worlds, that they were ignored and that their internal matters have been messed with, they'll be dropping out of United Planets like dandruff."

"What happened?" Ronny said.

Sid Jakes grumbled deprecation. "The conference has knocked off for the day and the delegates have melted away into their various embassies, to hotels, or to the homes of friends. The Holy Ultimate only knows where the Baron is. It'll be a neat trick finding him, if he doesn't want to be found."

## IV

When Ronny Bronston came in, in the morning, Irene Kasansky looked up from her desk, and said, in comparatively good humor, "Where've you been, Ronny? The commissioner's been asking for you."

Ronny said mildly, "I've been getting some sleep. Remember? Even Section G operatives have to do it occasionally."

She snorted, but not with her usual acidity. "Jetsam, jetsam. All I get around here is jetsam. Why I don't go drivel-happy . . ."

Ronny grinned at her, pushed through the door beyond her desk, turned left in the corridor and knocked at another door, which was inconspicuously lettered, *Ross Metaxa, Commissioner, Section G.* Ronald Bronston seldom entered here, without the realization coming over him, all over again, that behind this door was possibly the single most powerful man in United Planets, and that not one person in a million had ever heard of him. Ross Metaxa of Section G, the ultra-secret enforcement arm of the inner-workings of United Planets. Section G, whose unstated principle was that the ends justified the means: any means necessary to achieve the United Planets dream were acceptable. As always, when this thought came to him, Ronny Bronston shook his head. He had been raised in another ethic.

By his appearance, once would have assumed that the commissioner of Section G had not seen his bed the night before. Either that, or he had been on a monumental toot. He was red and slightly moist of eye, his clothes more disheveled than before. He looked up grumpily, when Ronny entered.

Sid Jakes was there, too, sprawled in a chair, his hands in his pockets, his face in its all but perpetual grin. Lee Chang Chu was also present, sitting demurely to one side of Metaxa's desk, her *cheongsam* dress emphasizing her oriental background.

Metaxa grunted. "Ronny. Good. We're just about to get underway. Drink?" He made a motion to the inevitable squat bottle that stood at his right hand.

Ronny shuddered. "That stuff? And this time of day?" He looked at the girl. "Hi, Lee Chang." So far as he knew every unmarried man in Section G was in love with the diminutive Chinese girl, despite the fact that she was possibly the most effective agent of them all, and had reached supervisor status, ranking the great majority.

She smiled her slow smile and nodded her greetings, as though too shy to speak out in this gathering of men.

Metaxa grunted, "Sid, bring Ronny up to date."

Sid chuckled happily. "Everything's going to pot. Whether or not we're going to keep the lid on this, even temporarily, is moot. We though we'd selected the two thousand most responsible chiefs of state of United Planets. Actually, what we've got is a madhouse. Hardly any two of them agree on what's to be done. At least a dozen have dropped out of UP."

Ronny stared at him. "Dropped out! But why? In this emergency . . ."

Metaxa interrupted. "They didn't wait long enough to consider the emergency. As soon as they heard that we had been violating Articles One and Two, they resigned."

Lee Chang Chu spoke for the first time. She said softly,

36

"Self-interest we shall always have with us. There's a sizable percentage of our species that would rather die, and bring down the whole race with them, than face the threat of having their political or religious institutions changed."

There was no refuting that.

Sid went on. "Goshen and some of the other hairy-chested planets want to declare war on the aliens. Right now." He laughed his pleasure at the idea. "We don't even know where they are located in the galaxy, but Goshen wants to declare war. On their own planet, of course, they've resisted the introduction of gunpowder. Afraid that the serfs they exploit might get uppity if there were weapons available capable of knocking over castle walls. But they want to declare war on some unknown aliens, who evidently have the neat trick of changing a whole world's atmosphere from nitrogen-oxygen, to poison gas, overnight. Oh, great." Sid chortled again.

"Get on with it, you laughing hyena," Metaxa grumbled.

Sid said, "Others want to sue for peace. How we can sue for peace is another mystery. Keeping in mind that even if we knew where they came from, we still have no particular reason to believe we could communicate. Or, if we could, that they'd be interested in doing so. But even that's not the end. A few of the member planets want to send missionaries. Missionaries, yet! If there's anything that'll irritate just anybody at all, it's bothering around with his religious institutions. Besides, who ever heard of missionaries being sent from a weaker to a stronger power. It's the stronger power that always beats weaker neighbors over the head with its missionaries."

Ronny said, thoughtfully, "What is our own stand? Section G has been aware of the problem for over a century. What *should* we do?"

Metaxa stirred in his chair. He growled, "For the most part, what we have been doing. That is, speeding up our own development by every means that we can. Scientifically, industrially, socio-economically. . . ."

Ronny frowned at him.

His chief scowled back. "We've got to push toward the optimum socio-economic system. . . ."

Ronny said mildly, "There are nearly as many ideas on what that is as you've got persons who have considered the question."

Sid chuckled.

Metaxa growled, "Please, no humor at this time of day. So far as we're concerned, the optimum social system is one under which the greatest number can exercise the greatest amount of each individual's ability. As much education as the individual can assimilate, all-out encouragement of unusual gifts, absolutely nothing so silly as industrial production cycles that allow such nonsense as unemployment, not to speak of anything as reactionary as featherbedding."

Lee Chang Chu said softly, "It is an optimum which has been realized on few planets, I am afraid."

The commissioner said, "At this point, we are aware that our potential enemy exists, though we are not in contact. But we haven't any reason to believe that he is aware of *our* existence. It is possible that we have another year, another century, another millennium before our cultures touch. Possible, but not probable. To the extent we can delay that meeting, we can be more happily prepared for it. That's our job. Delay, delay, delay, while man continues to advance." He looked at Ronny again.

"And that's where you come in."

Ronny Bronston was taken aback. "What?"

Sid chuckled his amusement.

Ross Metaxa reached his hand out for his Denebian tequila, while saying to Lee Chang, "You're the only one of us that's been to Phrygia. Brief Ronny on the place. That's why I called you in."

Lee Chang nodded demurely. "Are you acquainted with the derivation of the planet's name, Ronny?"

"I don't believe so."

"It was one of the early Greek states. Myth has a story about one of its kings, a cloddy named Midas who had an abnormal love of gold. He befriended Silenus . . ."

Sid put in, "I know that one. The god of drunks."

Lee Chang looked at him from the side of her eyes and went on. "And as a reward Dionysus gave him one wish. He chose the power to turn everything he touched into gold." She twisted her mouth in gentle mockery. "The ramifications are obvious."

She looked at Ronny again. "The name has a certain validity. Phrygia, I mean. The original colonists were a group which rebelled against the growth of what was then called the Welfare State. They were even more emphatic than usual. Many planets have been colonized by elements strong for, ah, free enterprise, and opposed to any interference at all by the state in the management of business—not to speak of democratic ownership of the means of production, distribution and communications. The colonists of Phrygia didn't even believe in common ownership of such things as the post office and highways, not . . ."

Ronny blinked at her. "How can you conduct a post office or . . ."

Sid chuckled. "Ronny, old man, you don't go far enough into history. Don't you remember the Pony Express and Wells Fargo? In the early days, mail was in the hands of private concerns. And quite a hash they made of it, too. And early toll roads and toll bridges were private, too."

"At any rate," Lee Chang went on, "the settlers of Phrygia were strong individualists and great believers in pragmatism. On Phrygia, it's each man for himself and the devil take the hindmost."

"Also," said Sid, "dog eat dog, never give a sucker an even break, and if I don't take advantage of this situation, somebody else will." He laughed.

Lee Chang said thoughtfully, "The characteristic also manifests itself in their interplanetary relations. The Phrygians are great entrepreneurs, great traders. More than once, less advanced member planets have had to evoke Article Two of the UP Charter to avoid being swallowed up, economically speaking, by the stutes from Phrygia." She allowed herself a slight smile. "I suspect, actually, that they are in considerable revolt against the existence of such a restraint. Given a free rein, Phrygia would be in full control of a considerable section of her part of our growing confederacy, in short order."

When she paused, Ronny looked at his superior. "What's this got to do with me?"

Metaxa had slugged back the drink he had poured. As he wiped the heel of his beefy hand over his mouth, he said, "Sid didn't bring you completely up to date. Yesterday, when we found out it was Baron Wyler, who had tipped off Interplanetary News, we sent out a call to have him picked up. Until we are able to concoct some mutually satisfactory plans to present to United Planets as a whole, we want to keep the existence of the aliens secret in order to minimize confusion. However, the good Baron has flown the coop."

Ronny stared at him. "He's gone? Where?"

"Evidently, back to Phrygia. He came to the conference in his own official yacht. Which is, by the way, at least as fast as any Space Forces cruiser, or public transportation. You won't be able to beat him back to his home planet, no matter how soon you start."

It was clearing up now. Ronny looked from one of them to the other. "You want me to go to Phrygia, eh? What do I do there?"

Ross scowled at him. "If we knew, then we wouldn't have to send as good a man. You play it by ear. Do what has to be done."

Ronny grunted at the left-handed compliment. "How big is our Section G force on Phrygia?"

Metaxa looked at Sid Jakes.

Sid was amused. "Only one man," he said. "And he's incognito. Operates under the guise of a member of the UP Department of Trade. The Phrygians are as stute as they come and evidently suspect the true nature of Section G. They don't want any of our operatives stirring around in their affairs."

Ronny came to his feet. "I suppose I'd better get under way." He hesitated. "What happened to Rita Daniels and Rosen?"

Sid shrugged. "We memorywashed them and sent them back to Interplanetary News. They can't complain. They've been violating Article Two in return for news beats."

Irene Kasansky had made the arrangements for his trip out to Phrygia. When Ronny issued forth from Metaxa's sanctum sanctorium, she had looked up at him from her multiple duties on phone screen and order box, at desk mike and auto-files.

"Got your marching orders, eh? Before they're through in there, there won't be an agent left on Mother Earth." She handed a slip of paper to him. "Your shuttle for Neuve Albuquerque leaves at six. You'll have only one hour stop-over. It's all on the paper there. Take care of yourself, Ronny."

It occurred to him only then, why Metaxa and Jakes had sent but one agent to Phrygia. Section G must be impossibly short of men in this crisis. Metaxa must have a thousand sore spots with which to deal. Metaxa had been right, up there on the podium, man was in the clutch and must soon alter all his most basic institutions, or he would be a sitting duck for the ultra-advanced aliens.

Ronny Bronston packed sparsely. He had no idea how long he might remain on the distant planet, which was his destination. It might be a matter of hours or years; he might spend the rest of his life there. However, if the stay were lengthy, he could augment his possessions on the spot. To date, he had no idea of what Phrygia climate or clothing styles might be. Why overload himself with non-essentials?

The roof of his apartment building was a copter-cab pickup point, and it took him little time to make his way to the Greater Washington shuttleport. Within three hours of his exit from Ross Metaxa's office, he was being lobbed over to the spaceport at Neuve Albuquerque.

Irene had made him reservations on an interplanetary liner, rather than assigning a Space Forces cruiser. More confortable than the military craft, of course, but not so fast. He shrugged. It was a long trip, and one to which he didn't look forward.

When Ronny Bronston had been a younger man, working in Population Statistics in New Copenhagen, had someone suggested that he wouldn't enjoy interplanetary travel, he would have thought the other mad. Getting into space was every earthborn boy's dream, and few there were who realized it. Long since, the authorities had taken measures to keep Earth's population from leaving wholesale. These days, when new planets were colonized, the colonists came from older settled planets, other than Earth. Earth, the source of man, could not spare its people. Its sole "industry" had at long last become the benevolent direction of human affairs, a super-government. More than four thousand man-populated worlds looked to it, in one degree or another, even those not members of United Planets.

However, no matter how strong the dream, no matter how wrapped up in interplanetary affairs, Ronny Bronston soon came to realize that the actual time involved in getting from one colonized planet to the next was the sheerest of boredom. All passenger activity in space was manufactured activity. There was little to do, certainly nothing to see, once the ship has gone into underspace.

One sits and reads. One plays battle chess, or other games. One talks with one's fellow passengers. One watches the Tri-Di tapes, if one is mentally of that level.

Thus it was, on the first day out, that Ronny Bronston made his way to the lounge, hoping that at least the craft was stocked with reading material new to him.

He sank into an auto-chair, as far as possible from the Tri-Di stage, and reached his hand for the stud, which would activate the reading tape listing, set into the chair's arm. His eye, however, hit upon the fellow passenger seated a few feet to his right.

He frowned, and said, "Don't we know each . . ."

and then broke it off. Of course. It was Rita Daniels, the Interplanetary News reporter. He hadn't recognized her at first, since she had been wearing a heavy makeup disguise—trying to look like the Supreme Matriarch, Harriet Dos Passos—when he had seen her last. Now, in her own guise, he realized that she was considerably younger than he had thought—and considerably more attractive.

She was blonde, a bit too slim, with a pert, slightly freckled face, and ignored current hair style in favor of a rather intricate ponytail arrangement. In spite of her pertness, there was another more elusive quality, a certain vulnerableness about her mouth. She was clad in a businesslike, inconspicuous crimson suit, and she obviously was of the opinion that this somewhat colorless young man was attempting to pick her up.

She said cooly, "I am afraid not"—and turned away.

*What in the name of the Holy Ultimate was she doing on this vessel?* The implication was obvious.

He snapped his fingers. "Citizeness Daniels. Interplanetary News."

She turned on him, her eyebrows high, in surprise. "I'm sorry. You do seem to know me. But . . . I'm afraid . . ."

It came to him suddenly that to reveal his true identity would put her on guard. However, he had an advantage. He knew she had been memorywashed. There was a period of at least twenty-four hours, probably more, of which she remembered nothing whatsoever, nor did her immediate superior, Rosen. It must be a confusing situation, he realized. But advantage, it was.

He said easily, smiling, "You remember me. Just yesterday."

She blinked, her eyes immediately alert. Without doubt, she was keen to take advantage of an opportunity to replace erased memories. "Oh, yes, of course, Citizen . . ."

He grinned at her, both on the surface and inwardly, in true amusement. "Smythe," he supplied. "Jimmy Smythe. I helped you out of that trouble with the bottle of guzzle and the traffic coordinator. Wow, were you drenched, eh?"

She stared at him blankly.

## V

"Where are you bound?" he said, the standard traveler's gambit. He was less apt to be suspect if he asked it.

She hesitated, then smiled. "End of the line, I suppose. All the way to Phrygia."

"Some special news story?"

This time the hesitation was longer, but the question was still the expected one anybody, knowing she was a reporter, would ask. She smiled ruefully, and said, "What else? And you?"

He projected embarrassment. "My job is supposed to be kind of secret. Orders are not to discuss it with anybody."

She laughed, obviously not caring. "I'll have to worm it out of you. Probably make a good newstape."

He grunted self-deprecation. "Hardly. Worst luck. It must be something, being with Interplanetary News. You must meet a lot of interesting people."

She looked at him, as though wondering if he were kidding. However, no matter how much of a yoke, he was probably better than no companionship at all, and it was a long trip. Besides, he knew at least something about what had happened to her during her twenty-four hour blackout.

"Well, yes," she drew out. "I suppose so. There's a lot of fun being on the *inside* of everything." She was wondering how she could get around to asking just what the circumstances were under which he had met her. Perhaps the blunt approach would do it. He didn't seem to be particularly stute, not to say devious. At most, there seemed to be a kind of sad sensitivity about him, as though he felt something in life was passing him by.

"How about a drink?" he suggested, looking down at the wine list in the chair's arm. He winced at the prices, as he knew an ordinary traveling salesman type might do.

"In space? Good heavens."

"I'll put it on the expense account," he said, with an air of gallantry. "Oiling up the press, or whatever they call it."

They settled for John Brown's Bodies, and he told her the one about feeling like you were moldering in your grave, came morning.

Then he said, "How do you mean, on the 'inside' of everything?"

She considered that. "Well, back when I was in school I decided that there were two kinds of people throughout the worlds. Those who were on the inside pertaining to everything that really counts, and those who were on the outside, and didn't have a clue. And I decided, then and there, I wanted to be an insider."

He sipped his drink and looked at her, his eyes guileless. "I'll bet you were in your sophomore year, when you thought that up," he said.

"Why . . . as a matter of fact, I suppose I was," she said. "How did you know?"

"I used to work in statistics," he said meaninglessly. He covered over. "But what is an example of being on the inside?"

She touched the tip of her slightly freckled nose, in a young girl's gesture, slightly incongruous on the part of an experienced news-hen. "Well, let's take one of the early examples. Have you ever heard of a man named Hearst?"

He had, but he said no.

"Well, Hearst was the owner of a newspaper chain back about the turn of the 20th Century. At that time, he supported a group that believed the United States was getting into the colony-grabbing game too late. He beat the drums for intervention in Cuba, where a great deal of American capital was invested, against Spain. The story is that he sent a photographer down to take pictures of the war. The photographer cabled that there wasn't any war. And Hearst cabled back, *You supply the photos, I'll supply the war.* And he continued to beat the drums. Not long after, the American battleship *Maine* was sunk in Havana harbor."

Ronny nodded. "I've often wondered who sank the *Maine*," he said.

She looked at him.

He said reasonably, "Obviously, it had to be one of three groups, the Cubans, the Spanish or the Americans. No one else was involved. Of them all, the Spanish had the least reason to sink it. The sad excuse for a war that followed was ample proof that they wanted to provoke no such scrap." He paused, then added thoughtfully, "I wonder if the ship was well insured."

"Look," she demanded, "who's being cynical here, you or me?"

He laughed, as though embarrassed. "Go on."

"So, pushed by Hearst and other drum beaters, President McKinley got increasingly tougher. Unfortunately, the Spanish didn't cooperate. Their queen ordered Cuban hostilities suspended, in an attempt to placate the Americans. They were doing all they could to keep the war from happening. However, Hearst and the other

48

drum beaters hardly mentioned her efforts. And McKinley ignored the fact that the potential enemy had already offered capitulation, when he addressed Congress asking for war measures. To wind it all up, the Spanish were clobbered. It was like taking candy from babes."

Ronny attempted to portray dismay. "So that's what it's like to be on the inside. You mean the press can actually influence the news."

She laughed at him in scorn. "My dear Citizen Smythe, the press today makes the news. We shape it to fulfill our own needs, to realize our own ideals, to build a better race."

He looked at her, wide-eyed, in complete sympathy. "The way you put it, it's absolutely inspiring."

She had his admiring interest now, and responded. "Take for instance," she explained, "some planet of which we don't approve. Suppose that three news items came out of there one day. The first mentions a new cure for cancer; the second, some startling statistics on industrial progress being made; the third mentions a riot by high school children, who overturn some copter-cabs in the streets and throw stones through some windows. What story do you think we put on the interplanetary broadcasts?"

"You mean the last one? Only the last one?"

"Why should we mention the other two?" she said reasonably.

"Well, doesn't it kind of involve freedom of speech, or of the press, or something?"

She scoffed at him. "It's our press, isn't it? The freedom consists of printing what we wish."

"Well, that isn't the way I should have put it. I mean, the right of the public to know . . . or something."

She scoffed again. "Let's have another of these. What

did you call them? This time we'll put it on Interplanetary News' swindle sheet." She dialed the drinks. "It's up to us, we who are on the inside, to decide what the public ought to know. They're a bunch of yokes, not up to making decisions."

Ronny thought about it. "Well, possibly the reason they're yokes, like you say, incapable of making competent decisions, is because they're improperly informed. But, anyway, that's the reason you're going to Phrygia, eh? Something really inside is going on."

She sipped the potent drink and scowled at him. "As a matter of fact, I don't know what's going on. But it's something very big. It involves Baron Wyler himself."

"Who's Baron Wyler?" Ronny said, trying to look as though he were trying to look interested.

She was stung by the fact that she didn't seem to be impressing him. "I can see you're not one of those insiders. The Baron is the most aggressive single man in UP. He's Supreme Commandant of Phrygia and Phrygia is the most aggressive planet in the system."

Ronny snorted. "What good does it do to be aggressive these days? Under United Planets, no member planet is allowed to interfere with any other. Where can your aggressiveness, go, besides inward?"

She opened her mouth to retort, then closed it suddenly. She looked into her drink. "These are strong, aren't they, Jerry?"

"Pretty strong, all right. In the auto-bars, they usually have a sign—only one to a customer."

She cocked her head to one side. "Oh, listen. That song." She wagged her head to it, setting her blonde ponytail aswing. It was coming from the Tri-Di stage at the other end of the lounge. "Do you dance?" she said.

"Well, a little. I'm not very good at this rock'n'swing stuff."

She stood up. "Neither am I. Let's try this, it's an old favorite of mine."

He took her in his arms and they joined half a dozen other couples on the small dance floor.

They had taken only a few steps before she said, tightly, "That's what I thought. You're carrying a shooter, aren't you?"

"I beg your pardon?"

She stopped dancing, turned and returned to her chair. She began to pick up her half-finished drink, but then sat it down again, decisively.

He lowered himself to his own seat, across from her, and looked into her eyes.

She said bitterly, "It's that ineffective air of yours. Who are you from?"

He shook his head.

She asked, "How did you know my name?"

"Like I said, I met you yesterday."

"Yes. You also said your name was Jimmy Smythe, and then managed to forget that, not correcting me, when I called you 'Jerry'."

She had him there. Ronny had to laugh aloud.

She said, bitterly, "You look smarter when you laugh. How did you know my name?"

Ronny shook his head, as though sorry she wouldn't believe him.

She said, "If you met me yesterday, then you probably have something to do with the Commissariat of Interplanetary Affairs."

"Why should that follow?" he asked mildly.

"Because yesterday"—she hesitated, then plunged on—"through a tip given us by . . . one of our informants, I went to the Octagon, on an assignment from Dave Rosen. I was memorywashed there, and, now, can't even remember the assignment."

Ronny played it out. "Why not ask this—what was his name? Rosen?—what he sent you for?"

"He was memorywashed, too, as you undoubtedly are aware."

He shrugged. "I thought that was very illegal. Who did it?"

"How could we know? I told you, we were memorywashed."

Ronny scowled puzzlement at her. "Well, why not just check back with your informant and find out what tip you were working on?"

"That's what I'm doing," she said, still bitterly. "Unfortunately, he's gone all the way to Phrygia." She got up, preparatory to stomping off. "And don't ask me why we don't simply ultra-wave him. All-Planet Press, the Bureau of Investigation and who knows who else, would be listening in. Good-bye, Jerry!"

"Jimmy," Ronny said mildly. "Sure you wouldn't like another drink I was really beginning to enjoy our talk, about being inside and all."

Rita Daniels wasn't as much of a lightweight as his first encounter on the spaceline with her might have indicated. She avoided him for two days, then showed up at his table in the passenger's mess, while he was finishing off some fruit dessert.

He began to come to his feet, but she slid into a chair before he could invite her.

"Your name is Ronald Bronston," she informed him. "And you're an operative for Ross Metaxa in that Section G mystery outfit. In fact," she added snappishly, "you're one of his top hatchet-men. I must say, it's hard to believe."

He said calmly, "You Interplanetary News people have your resources, haven't you?"

"What do you want with me?" she asked flatly.

"Nothing," he told her. He didn't like this. If he hadn't been a flat, he would have let the girl alone. Evidently, she had an in with Baron Wyler, or, at least, Interplanetary News did, and she through that organization. Now the Baron would be informed that Agent Bronston was on his way, and the Baron didn't cotton to Section G.

"Then what are you doing following me?"

"I wasn't aware that I was, Citizeness Daniels. We're simply on the same vessel." He twisted his mouth ruefully. "Why don't we start all over again?"

"And you continue to pump me? No thanks. Do you deny that you're going to Phrygia?"

He thought about it. "No. I don't deny that. But, you know, I could reverse the question. Why are you following me?"

"Don't be silly."

"Well, we're on the same spacecraft and you don't deny you're going to Phrygia."

She stood again, abruptly. "I don't know why I was memorywashed, but, obviously, something big is in the wind and my job is to find out what."

He murmured mildly. "So that Interplanetary News will be inside, eh?"

She glared at him. "And, don't be too sure that Section G won't be outside."

He wasn't too sure at all.

A few hours before estimated coming out time, he approached the captain's private quarters and looked into the door's screen. He said, "Ronald Bronston, requesting an interview with Captain Henhoff."

The screen said, "The Captain is busy. Could you state your business?"

He brought forth his badge and held it to the screen. "Important matters involving the Bureau of Investigation."

In a few moments, the door opened. Ronny stepped through.

Captain Henoff's quarters were moderately ample, considering that this was, after all, a spacecraft. He was seated at a desk, going through reports, a junior officer across from him, taking orders.

The captain, frowning, said, "Citizen Bronston? What can I do for you? Frankly, I am afraid I've never heard of Section G of the Bureau of Investigation."

Ronny looked at the junior officer. "May I speak to you privately?"

The frown had become a testy scowl. However, the skipper said, "Howard, go on out into the corridor. I'll call you."

Howard got up, looked at Ronny, shrugged and left.

The captain said, "Well?"

Ronny laid it on the line. "We'll be coming out of underspace and setting down at Phrygia in a matter of hours. I'm on a special mission. I have reason to believe an attempt will be made at the spaceport to apprehend me. I want to be smuggled off the ship in some manner."

Captain Henhoff leaned back in his swivel chair. "That's asking a lot."

Ronny said, "I suggest you get in touch with your superiors and ask whether or not you should cooperate with Section G."

Henhoff looked at him for long moment. He said finally, "I suppose that won't be necessary." He thought about it. "They use pilots at Phrygia. Usually, three men pick us up in orbit and supervise setting us down. When we've finally set down, a spaceport auto-floated picks them up and runs them back to the spacepilot quarters, while the ship is still going through quarantine procedures. You can leave with them. I'll see that one of the men fixes you up in a uniform like the pilots wear to get you by. Think that would do it?"

"It should," Ronny nodded. "Thanks, Captain."

"You're not doing anything against the Phrygian government, are you? I don't want to get into trouble with that gang."

"Of course not. I've shown you my credentials. You don't think the Department of Interplanetary Justice goes about meddling in the affairs of member planets of UP, do you?" Ronny was very righteous.

"No. Of course not."

He left the liner in the spacepilot's auto-floater, as provided; the others couldn't have cared less. They probably figured he was some Tri-Di entertainment star, beating the fans out of an opportunity to give him the rush, when the regular passengers disembarked.

His precautions had been well merited.

At the foot of the spaceliner's disembarking ladder, he noted, stood three brawny, though inconspicuously dressed men. He didn't have to look at their feet to know their calling.

The Supreme Commandant's welcoming committee for visiting Section G operators. Citizeness Daniels was doing her best to make certain that whilst Interplanetary News got inside, the Bureau of Investigation didn't.

# VI

The auto-floater left him off at the spacepilot's quarters, and Ronny Bronston started off up the street immediately. He wanted to get out of the vicinity of the spaceport as soon as possible. He imagined that it would take a half hour or so before the Phrygians realized that he had gotten through their fingers. He didn't know what their instructions were: Whether they had meant simply not to allow him to disembark, or whether he was to be picked up and questioned by Phrygian authorities. Probably the latter. Undoubtedly, they had their own version of Scop. Nobody, but nobody, stood up under questioning these days.

He had none of the local means of exchange, whatever it was. His instructions had been to go immediately to the United Planets building and get in touch with Section G operative Phil Birdman, who would check him out on the local situation.

The auto-floater he had been in with the spacepilots had been similar to those on Earth, and were fairly general on the more advanced planets. He assumed there were taxis, of some sort or another, and kept his eyes open for something resembling a stand, having no idea of how the locals summoned such a vehicle.

He was struck by a certain *sameness* about this city. It was, he knew, named Phrygia and was the capital city of the planet of the same name.

The sameness, he decided—even as he strode briskly up a shopping street—came from the fact that so many of the buildings, vehicles, signs, traffic indicators and what not, were those of Earth, Avalon, Shangri-La, Catalina and Jefferson—the most advanced worlds. Evidently, Phrygia was quick to pick up any discoveries and developments pioneered elsewhere. Well, that was commendable.

There was one thing though. The average person in the street seemed to have a drab quality. Not one person in a hundred seemed up to the styles and general appearances of well-being, that one would find on Earth or Shangri-La. Yes, a gray drabness that you couldn't quite put your finger upon. They seemed well-fed and healthy enough, however.

He came to what would seem to be a cab stand, and stood, for a moment, looking at the first vehicle in line. He wanted to avoid asking questions and thus branding himself a stranger.

Well, he could only try. If the cab weren't fitted to take instructions in Earth Basic, he would be out of luck.

He opened the door and slipped into a rear seat. He made himself comfortable, and said into the screen, "The United Planets Building."

No trouble. The vehicle started up and edged itself into the street traffic.

The UP Building, he found, he could have easily walked to. It was less than a mile from the spaceport.

There were two Space Marines on guard at the door. Ronny Bronston called out to one of them.

The marine marched over and scowled down into the car.

Ronny flashed his badge. "I just came from the spaceport and have no local exchange. Can you pay the cab off for me?"

"Oh. Yes, sir. Certainly. They use credit cards here,

sir." The marine brought one from his pocket and held it to the cab's screen. The door automatically opened.

Ronny stepped out and said, "Now, quickly, take me to Citizen Phil Birdman."

The marine blinked. "Yes, sir." He turned and marched off, Ronny following.

The suite of offices was lettered simply, *Interplanetary Trade*.

Ronny said, "Thanks. I'll have that cab fare returned to you."

"Not necessary, sir," the space soldier said stiffly. "We're on unlimited expense account." He did an about-face and was off.

Ronny looked after him for a moment. How does it feel to be a professional soldier, when there hasn't been a war for centuries? He grunted sourly. Perhaps the soldier would be practicing his trade before long.

He opened the door and entered into a reception room. He walked over to the screen and said, "Ronald Bronston, Section G. To see Phil Birdman."

A door beyond opened immediately and a very dark-complected man, in his mid-forties, well over six feet tall and with a startlingly handsome face, came hurrying out, hand extended.

"Come in!" he said. "Holy Jumping Zen, it's been two years since I've seen a fellow agent from Section G."

Ronny ignored the hand. He brought his wallet out and showed his badge. He touched it with a finger and the badge glowed silver.

Birdman laughed, said, "Okay, okay, if you want to play it formal." He fished his own wallet out and displayed his badge. He touched it with a finger, and like Bronston's it shone brightly.

Ronny stuck out his hand for the shake, grinning self-deprecation.

Birdman cocked his head on one side. "Something must be up."

"Yes," Ronny said. "Let's get out of here."

The tall dark man looked at him. "Get out to where? Come on in the office and we'll have some firewater."

Ronny shook his head impatiently. "I'm already on the run. They'll probably be here any minute. Surely you've got an ultimate hideout—just in case."

"Wait'll I get my shooter," the other clipped. He hurried back into the inner office, returned in moments, shrugging a shoulder holster into a more comfortable position beneath his jacket.

"This way."

He led Ronny through a series of doors and halls, finally emerging at the back of the building. There was a row of hovercars. Birdman slid into one, a speedy-looking model. Ronny slipped into the seat beside him.

"We're not going very far in this, are we?" Ronny growled. "If it's yours, it's spotted."

"Of course," Birdman grunted. "Who are you working with?" His hand maneuvered the vehicle out of the parking area and into the traffic stream.

"Directly under the Old Man," Ronny said.

"Oh? And Sid Jakes? How's Sid?"

"Chuckling his fool head off," Ronny said.

They spoke no more for the next fifteen minutes, during which time Phil Birdman put on a show of how to lose a possible tail and leave no possible trail behind, in a big city. They dropped his car after a few miles, sending it back to the UP Building. They took a cab for a time. Then they got out and walked. They took a rolling road for a time. They took a pneumatic. Then they walked some more.

Finally, in a residential area, they entered a house. It seemed deserted. They entered a closet. The closet was an elevator.

When they left the elevator, they were in a Spartan apartment, well-equipped from the Section G gimmick department, and from Communications and Weaponry.

Ronny looked about and whistled approvingly through his teeth. "Nice setup, considering you're only one man here."

Birdman nodded. "I'm going to have to brace Sid Jakes on that. We need a bigger staff. Phrygia is more important than they seem to think back there in the Octagon." He headed for a manual bar. "Now how about that firewater?"

"Firewater?" Ronny said.

Phil Birdman grinned at him. "Ugh, guzzle, you pale-faces call it. I'm from Piegan."

Ronny frowned in memory. "Oh, yes," he said. "Colonized by Amerinds. Mostly Blackfeet and Sioux. Die-hards, who still wanted to get away from the whiteman and go back to the old tribal society. Setup, kind of a primitive communism, based on clan society."

"That's the way it started," Birdman nodded. "How about pseudo-whiskey?" At Ronny's nod, he added, "And water?" He finished the drinks and returned with them.

Ronny was already seated. He took the drink and said, "How did it work out?"

"Piegan? Terribly. You can't go back, no matter how strong the dream."

"So what happened?"

Birdman grinned at him, wryly. "Section G happened.

A few of the boys turned up and subverted our institutions. Best thing that every happened. We've still got an Indian society, but we're rapidly industrializing. Couple of more decades and we'll be at least as advanced as Phrygia, here."

Ronny drank half of the pseudo-whiskey down. "If any of us are around, a couple of decades from now."

The big Indian looked at him. "I knew it was something important," he said.

Ronny nodded and briefed the other operative on recent developments.

Their drinks were finished by the time he was through. His host got up to get new ones. "And now?" he asked.

Ronny shrugged. "My assignment isn't particularly important. Just one phase of the whole. Ross Metaxa wants me to take what steps I can and keep Baron Wyler from sounding off about the Octagon's plans to speed up the amalgamation of United Planets and all other human settled worlds. From what this mopsy, Rita Daniels, tells me, the Baron has been playing footsie with Interplanetary News."

"Footsie, yet," Birdman snorted. "Baron Wyler *is* Interplanetary News."

Ronny gaped at him. "What are you talking about?"

"I told you we need a larger staff here. There's a lot cooking that's going to have to come right before Metaxa's eyes. I'm working on the report right now. At any rate, Baron Wyler owns communications on Phrygia. All communications. And he also controls Interplanetary News. Who did you think owned it?"

"It never occurred to me to wonder. I realize, of course, that we've got every kind of socio-economic system ever dreamed up, through the centuries, at one place or another in United Planets; but I didn't think in terms of an organization as strong as Interplanetary News being privately owned. Certainly not by one individual."

"It's not exactly one individual," the Indian growled. "More like a family, and the Baron's the head of the family."

He made a face. "I'd better give you some background. You were right, when you said UP has every socio-economic system ever dreamed up by man, on one planet or the other. It also has a lot of crisscrosses."

Ronny frowned at him.

Birdman explained. "Take communism. We've got planets, such as my own Piegan used to be, that practice primitive tribal communism. Then we've got planets of 'purists,' who have attempted to build a society such as Marx and Engels originally had in mind back in 1848. Then we've got a sample or two of communism, as Lenin saw it; then, one or two as DeLeon adapted socialism to America; and, at least one on the Stalinist conception —that's a *real* honey—and one, I can think of, based on Trotsky's heresy. And Mao, the Chinese. And Tito, remember Tito?"

"No," Ronny said, "but you've made your point. There's a lot of confusion on just what communism is."

The Indian was nodding. "Yes. Well, the crisscross on this planet is a doozy. You might call it industrial feudalism. Kind of a classical capitalism gone to seed. Kind of free enterprise without either freedom, or, except for a handful, any enterprise. You see, they got to the point where the wealth of Phrygia is in the hands of less than one percent of the population. The means of production, distribution, communications, the farms, the mines, the whole shebang—all owned and controlled by comparatively few families."

Ronny grunted. "In any society, a good man gets to the top."

"Or loses his scalp trying," Birdman agreed. "If he can't, he tries to change the society. Well, they have one fairly workable way of getting around that on Phrygia. Any real stute that comes along, gets adopted into one of the big families. The Romans used to do the same thing; Octavius was an adopted son of Caesar.

"But to get on with it. There's evidently no end to the desire for wealth and the power it brings. A millionaire wants to become a billionaire and a billionaire wonders how it'd be to have a trillion. Far, far beyond the point where his own needs are completely satisfied, the stute with a power complex continues to accumulate more wealth, more power. It might not make sense to you and me, but there it is. Well, Baron Wyler has about outgrown Phrygia. He's looking for new worlds to conquer, and I've a sneaking suspicion he doesn't expect to allow United Planets to stand in his way. In fact, it didn't even start with the present Baron. The dream had evidently been in his family, and probably other industrial feudalistic families here, for several generations. Interplanetary News is just one of the projects designed to help pave the way."

Ronny was staring at him.

The Indian chuckled sourly. "Sounds unbelievable, eh? Well, in spite of the far-out nature of this super-loose confederation of ours, United Planets is still basically a republic. Whatever the home government of each planet, in the UP it has one voice, one vote, no more. But there's no particular reason why man, in his eruption into space, has to remain a republican. Given a strong enough ambition on the part of a few fellas like our good

Baron, and what's to prevent an empire from being established?"

Ronny was shaking his head. "To many would fight."

The other nodded in agreement. "That's what's baffled me. Something is going on. Something the Baron is counting upon to give him such an edge over the other strong worlds, which would ordinarily resist his ambitions, that he'd prevail."

Ronny Bronston thought about it for a long moment, staring down into his glass. He said finally, "I suppose it's about time I got in touch with this Baron Wyler. Have you got a Section G communicator handy?"

"Over there."

Ronny sat at the indicated desk. The device was about the size of a woman's vanity case, and was propped up now so that the small screen was immediately before the operative. He activated it.

"Ronald Bronston," he said. "I want to report to Supervisor Jakes, soonest."

He sat there, saying nothing, until Sid Jakes' grinning face appeared on the screen.

"Hi, Ronny." He chuckled. "On Phrygia, eh? How's that redskin coming along?"

Ronny said, "That redskin is evidently a one-man task force. He's dug up the fact that Baron Wyler controls Interplanetary News and is evidently prettying up a scheme to unite UP . . ."

"Well, isn't that what we want to do?"

". . . under his leadership. Possibly, I should say, under his dictatorship."

The supervisor scoffed. "Neat trick, if he could pull it off."

"Evidently, he has some reason to believe he can."

Sid Jakes looked at him thoughtfully. "Get a complete report on this, soonest, Ronny."

"Phil Birdman's just about got it finished. Meanwhile, would it be possible for you to put through an order making me a plenipotentiary extraordinary from UP to the Supreme Commandant of Phrygia?"

"Have you gone drivel-happy, old boy?"

"No. The Baron's got his heavies out looking for me. I want to face him, but not on the kind of basis he evidently has in mind. I want some weight to throw around."

Jakes thought about it some more. "All right. Within twenty-four hours, you'll be a special mission from the President of UP to Baron Wyler. You'll have to play it from there. Dream up your own idea of what the mission is. Wyler won't dare touch you, with such a commission." He grinned. "This oughta be a neat trick."

He faded from the screen.

Ronny turned back to his companion.

Birdman said, "I'm not sure I like this. Wyler's feeling his oats. He's getting near the point where he's ready to take action. I don't think he's afraid of the Commissariat of Interplanetary Affairs."

Ronny shrugged. "The way you brought me here, to this hideout, I couldn't find it again. So even though he slips me Scop, I can't betray you. For myself, I'm no big loss. If I don't get away from him, again, there's not much he can get out of me that he doesn't already know. Now, let's get about the job of outfitting me properly to be a plenipotentiary from the President to the Baron. Sid is going to radio through to Wyler that I am to appear."

## VII

If Ronny Bronston had thought the surface buildings of
the nadirscraper, which housed the Interplanetary News
in Greater Washington, were ostentatious, he could only
admit he had had little upon which to base his opinion—
comparatively.

Baron Wyler's official residence was some ten kilome-
ters outside the Phrygia city limits. At first, the Section G
agent couldn't place the theme; but it began to come to
him, when his limousine—driven by a United Planets
Space Forces marine, in dress uniform, with another
seated beside him—was stopped at a gate by a squad of
men in an armor of yesteryear and in short linen tunics.
They were armed with spears, swords buckled to their
sides.

The driver said from the side of his mouth, "You're
getting the full official greeting, sir. Ordinarily, we
could've driven inside."

Six of the guards stood at rigid attention, spear butts
grounded. An officer, his breastplate of gold, approached
the heavy hovercar, and came to the salute.

He said, "Hail the Plenipotentiary from the United
Planets!"

Maintaining his dignity, Ronny nodded.

The officer said, "If your Excellency will alight, you will
be conducted to audience with the Supreme Commandant."

Evidently, his two marines were going to be left here
at the gate. Ronny mentally shrugged. He was already in

the Baron's hands. Let them bounce the ball. He left the car.

In a clatter and a small cloud of dust, a chariot, pulled by three enormous white horses, came speeding forth. Ronny blinked at it. He had seen chariots in illustrations, and in historic Tri-Di shows, but never in actuality.

The driver pulled the horses to a rearing halt, only a few feet from him.

The officer said, not a flicker of expression on his face, "If His Excellency will mount. . . ."

Ronny Bronston looked at his marines from the side of his eyes. They remained expressionless as well. He wondered vaguely if they would have pulled this gimmick had he been an eighty year old man. Well, there was nothing for it. He jumped up into the wheeled vehicle and grasped the edge, next to the driver.

They were off in a clatter.

The setting was beginning to come to him. The double-headed ax motif, the bulls in fresco and statuary. Once, as a boy, his father had taken him to the so-called Palace of Minos, at Knossos on Crete. Baron Wyler had obviously drawn upon the reconstructions of Sir Arthur Evans in building his residence. The British archaeologist had notoriously exercised his imagination in the reconstruction; but many a Cretean must have turned in his grave at this version of a palace of the four thousand year old civilization.

They clattered up a broad ramp, Ronny Bronston hanging on for life, and came to a rearing halt before an entrada flanked with highly colorful columns, which started narrow at the bottom and widened at the roof.

There was another guard unit, clad in the costume of Knossos, at the entry. A full twenty of them here. They came to the salute.

An officer stepped forward, came to attention.

"The Supreme Commandant sends greetings to His Excellency, the Plenipotentiary from United Planets."

Ronny stepped down from the chariot, looked at the driver bitterly. Inaudibly he muttered. "Do you have a license to operate that thing?"

"Thanks," he said to the officer. "I would like to see the Baron immediately."

"His instructions are to bring you to his quarters upon arrival, Your Excellency."

He turned and marched, stiff legged, into the building. Ronny followed.

As at the Interplanetary News building in Greater Washington, the resemblance to the ancient past fell off immediately in the interior. The officer's costume seemed doubly ludicrous among the hosts of guards, messengers, secretaries and officials, all garbed in modern dress.

Two guards, fish-cold of eye, stood before an elevator door, one behind a device of switches and screens. Ronny assumed he was being given an electronic frisk. Well, they'd find him clean. It would have been ridiculous to think he could approach the ruler of Phrygia armed.

The elevator opened and the officer accompanying him gestured. Ronny entered alone, the door closed and the car dropped.

Then the door reopened, and even before Ronny Bronston could step out, the tall, heavy-set man there—his face beaming—reached for his hand.

"Ronald Bronston!" he said heartily. "Your Excellency, I've been waiting for you!"

He was at least as tall as Phil Birdman, but would have outweighed the Indian by fifty pounds. He carried his weight well; gracefully, might be the word. He moved as a trained pugilist moves, or perhaps one of the larger cats. His charm reached out and embraced you, all but suffocatingly. His face was open, friendly; his eyes, blue and wide-set; his nose, the arched Hapsburg nose, giving an aristocratic quality that only his overwhelming friendliness could dissipate.

*He could only be,* Ronny realized, *Baron Wyler, Supreme Commandant of the Planet Phrygia, and, were Phil Birdman correct, would-be dictator of this sector of the galaxy.*

Ronny let his hand be pumped, admittedly taken aback. He realized now that, although he had never seen even a photo of the Baron, he had built up a ficticious picture of him. *Yes, the picture,* he admitted in sour realization, *had nothing to do with reality.* Among other things, far from being middle-aged or even an elderly Prussian type, the Baron was little older than Ronny, himself.

Ronny Bronston hated to be touched by another man —other than perhaps a quick handshake—however, he suffered now his host to place an arm around his shoulders and lead him to as comfortable a room as the Section G agent could remember ever having been in. It was a man's room. A small but complete bar to one side. A number of large, well-used chairs and couches. Racks of books that, even at a distance, looked interesting and oft-handled. Good, well-chosen, not necessarily expensive, paintings on the walls. A fireplace.

*A fireplace,* Ronny thought. *At this distance down into the Earth's crust?* He wondered vaguely what effort must have gone into devising a manner of dispelling smoke and fumes.

The Baron was at the bar. "May I suggest this departure on the wines of the Rhine and Moselle? One of my ancestors imported the Riesling grape to Phrygia. Local soil conditions were somewhat different; but I trust you will find a lightness and bouquet not at all unpleasing." Even as he spoke, he was pouring from a very long necked bottle into two delicate crystal glasses.

Ronny found himself seated in one of the chairs, glass in hand. The Baron was across from him and now picked up a small sheaf of papers from a coffee table.

He read aloud. "Ronald Meredith Bronston, 32. Born in Luana, Hawaii. Parents, Michael L. Bronston, and Pauline Meredith. Studied, ummm, ummm, finished education at University of Stockholm . . . ummm, ummm, at age of twenty-six took position at New Copenhagen in the Population Statistics Department. Was discovered by Bureau of Investigation scouts and jockeyed into Section G. . . ."

Ronny stared at him. "*Jockeyed*," he protested. "I applied for a position that would take me overspace and was lucky . . ."

Baron Wyler chuckled at him magnanimously. "My dear Bronston, no luck is involved in getting into our friend Metaxa's Section G. Not one human being in a million qualifies. Were you a bit more privy to the inner workings of your ultra-ultra cloak and dagger organization, you would know that at any given time at least a hundred of Metaxa's picked men are scouting out potential agents. You were probably selected as far back as when you were in high school."

Wyler's eyes went back to the report. "But to go on with it. Given first assignment with Supervisor Lee Chang Chu and, as a result, was made full agent. . . . Umm, umm, worked with distinction on the planets Kropotkin, Avalon and Palermo. Has become one of Supervisor Jakes' most trusted field men. Height, weight, ummm, fingerprints, eye pattern, skull measurements." The Baron looked up. "Some of these statistics come directly from Section G files."

"All right," Ronny said in resignation. "You've made your point. You have a rather complete dossier on me."

The Baron put down the report and turned on his charm with a smile. "So we can dispense with preliminaries and get to the point."

Ronny said, "The point being that the Supreme Commandant of the Planet Phrygia is ambitious to encroach upon the sovereignty of fellow worlds belonging to the United Planets."

"Which is one way of putting it." The Baron nodded agreeably. "Tell me, Bronston, what is the eventual goal of this United Planets to which you have devoted your life?"

"The advancement of the human race!"

"Neatly summed up in but six words. But, my dear Bronston, man has made his advances down through the ages in a wide variety of methods. Your knowledge of history must be such that you recognize the contributions of strongmen who have arisen in time of need. The democratic principle does not always apply."

Ronny said sharply, "My studies have led me to believe that man makes his greatest advances under conditions of freedom."

"An example?"

The Section G agent groped for a good one. "The Athens of the Golden Age. The Athenian democracy nourished a culture such as had never been seen before, nor since."

Baron Wyler chuckled. "My dear Bronston, have you never heard of the strongman, Pericles? Besides, calling the Athenian society a democracy is somewhat stretching a point, is it not? For every Athenian citizen free to pursue the arts and sciences, there were a dozen slaves, or more, kept in complete subjugation. Come now, do you contend that if these slaves—who did the drudgery necessary to maintain the leisure of the Athenian citizens—had been given their freedom, been given complete equality, that the Golden Age could have been?"

Ronny looked at him. The Baron was obviously no fool.

The Baron got up, brought the bottle from the bar and refreshed the glasses. The Section G agent was no connoisseur of wine, but, admittedly, this was the most pleasant beverage he could remember drinking. He wondered if it was available on Earth.

The Baron said, "Let me use a somewhat more recent example of strongman versus the mob."

"I wasn't exactly advocating mob rule."

"Indeed? However, remember when the Egyptian Nasser seized power in his country, oh, somewhere about the middle of the 20th Century? His nation had been a backward one, dominated by the big powers, ignored in the world's councils. When he took over the Suez Canal, all prophesied that the waterway would soon be silted up and impassable. Instead, within a few years, traffic had doubled. Borrowing, begging, securing funds and techniques from every source he could find, he began to industrialize, to irrigate, to find new potentials in his desert country. His soldiers were sent out to fill up the wells in thousands of native communities, supposedly a crime beyond understanding in a desert land. They filled them up and forced the fellahin to dig new wells in places where the water would not be contaminated with sewage. He sent soldiers out and rounded up the children and forced them into schools. Children that otherwise would have been taught nothing further than a few suras from the Koran. These were but a few things done by strongman Nasser."

Ronny was scowling at him.

The Baron twisted his mouth in deprecation. "At the same time, and on the same continent, the newly emerged nation, the Congo, seemed unable to find an equivalent of Nasser. Instead, in an atmosphere of pseudo-democracy, they went from one barbarism to the next, going backward, rather than progressing. Come now, Citizen Bronston, don't you think conditions sometimes call for a strongman?"

Ronny put his glass down. Thus far, he had been satisfied to hold his peace, if only to see just how the other was going to bounce the ball.

Now he said, "Interpreting history isn't my field. I do know this, as Metaxa said, the human race is in the clutch. This is not the time for would-be strongmen to try to seize control of worlds other than their own. We can't afford the time, nor the energies involved in interplanetary war. And, please don't attempt to put over the idea that you, or anyone else, could form an empire from the largely individualistic United Planets, without war. Baron Wyler, you saw that charred body of the intelligent alien life form. You heard what Ross . . ."

The Baron held up a hand to restrain him. He nodded, still agreeable. "Indeed I did. And I was surprised that the estimable Commissioner was in possession of it. However, we could have shown him better examples."

"Better examples?"

The Baron reached out and touched a switch on the coffee table. One wall of the room clouded, then became a giant screen.

The Baron fiddled with a small dial set into the table.

On the screen, there faded in an extensive laboratory. At least a dozen white-smocked men were working about an operating table. The Baron turned another dial, zooming in on the scene.

Ronny sucked in his breath. Those on the screen were dissecting two bodies of what were obviously specimens of the tiny life form Metaxa had deep frozen.

Another turn of the dial. A new room, more extensive than the last. At least several thousand men—technicians and mechanics—were working away at various benches, on various pieces of equipment: the nature of which, Ronny couldn't even guess.

The Baron said wryly, "They're trying to figure out the use of some of the devices, weapons or whatever, that we've gleaned from the alien planets." He snorted his deprecation. "What if you took a squad of Neanderthal men and set them down in a 25th Century laboratory in the midst of all the products that century produced? What do you think they might accomplish?"

Ronny, his eyes bugging still, said, "Is there that much difference?"

"At least," the Baron told him. "However, as our good Metaxa pointed out at the conference, this culture is not the one we must confront. This culture was destroyed by one beyond."

Ronny nodded. "That is the basic point, Baron Wyler. That is why the human race doesn't have the time to bother with ambitious men of the caliber of the Supreme Commandant of Phrygia. We know nothing at all about the culture beyond."

"Oh, I wouldn't say that," the Baron said easily. "A taste more wine?"

He had Ronny staring again. "What do you mean by that?"

The Baron waggled a finger at him. "You see, my dear

Bronston, we are far, far beyond Section G and its well-intentioned plans to preserve the race. Some time ago, long before the Space Forces exploration force located the alien planets, Phrygian cruisers had found them. Properly masked, of course, we were able to descend and explore. My laboratories have been working on the equipment, and even the bodies of the aliens, as you have seen. We found a few under conditions which had preserved them."

"But you said something about the power beyond."

The Baron nodded. "Yes. Our little aliens left enough in the way of photographs to indicate part of what we're up against."

"Photographs?"

"Both still photographs and also a tape that one of my more brilliant young men has been able to project. It would seem that our little aliens actually landed upon at least one of the beyond culture's planets."

For the last half hour the Baron had been throwing curves faster than Ronny Bronston found himself capable of catching. Now he blurted, "What in the world is the other culture like?"

"Fantastically advanced. Among other items, it would seem they have matter conversion units that can make anything out of anything else. It would seem they have fusion reactors, and, hence, unlimited power. Oh yes, an unbelievably advanced technology."

"What do they look like?"

The Baron paused. "Just a moment." He played with his screen dials again, said something into an order box. The screen clouded, went clear once more.

On it was an incredibly handsome man. He was dressed in nothing more than brief shorts and sandals. He had a golden-brown coloration, was of bodily perfection seldom seen, and then only among physical culture perfectionists who spend a lifetime achieving it. There was no indication that he was aware of being photographed.

"Who's that?" Ronny said blankly.

"That's one of your aliens."

"Alien! That's a *man*."

"Ummm," the Baron said. "There's just one thing in which he differs from man as we know him."

He paused for effect. "These aliens don't seem to be intelligent."

## PART TWO

## VIII

If Baron Wyler had suddenly metamorphosed into a gigantic butterfly, he could hardly have surprised Ronny Bronston more.

"Not *intelligent?*" he protested. "A moment ago you said they had an unbelievably advanced technology. Fusion reactors and matter conversion units aren't exactly the products of unintelligent minds."

The Baron looked at him strangely. "Can we be so sure? Have you ever considered some of the things insects accomplish? However, neither as individuals nor as units—such as beehives or anthills—do we think of insects as intelligent. But the analogy isn't too good. A moment, please."

He got up, walked over to a wall screen and said something into it, then returned.

"You noted, of course, how humanoid our Dawnman was?"

"Humanoid?" Ronny blurted. "That was a *man.*"

"Perhaps." There was still a strange element in the Baron's voice.

The screen on one of the room's doors said, "Academecian Count Felix Fitzjames, on orders to see the Supreme Commandant."

"Enter," the Baron said.

He made off-hand introductions, then said to Ronny

Bronston, "The Count has been specializing in this particular aspect of the matter. Undoubtedly, he will be pleased to enlighten you." He turned to the Count. "The matter of the nature of the Dawnmen."

"Dawnmen?" Ronny said.

The Academecian, who was an elderly scholar and somewhat nervous in the presence of his ultimate superior, said, "Undoubtedly, a misnomer, but one that has come into common usage among we who are working on the project. One hypothesis is that these aliens are the original *Homo sapiens*, that Earth was seeded from one of their planets."

Baron Wyler said affably, "Sit down, my dear Count."

The Count nervously sat, remaining on the edge of his chair.

Ronny said, "That's ridiculous. Earth is the origin of man."

The other nodded, apologetically. "Most likely, Your Excellency; however, there are those among us who think otherwise. You are undoubtedly aware of the theory that would evolve upon various planets. The fact that he stands erect, that his eyes are so placed, that he has a voicebox, so many of the other factors that go to make up the entity, man—all have good reason for having evolved, and given similar situations would evolve on similar worlds as on Earth."

"I've heard the theory," Ronny begrudged. "I haven't thought too much about it."

"Most authorities don't," the other bobbed his head agreeably. "However, there are certain factors that give credence to *Homo sapiens'* evolution elsewhere. For instance, we know that the earliest man-like creatures, *Zinjanthropus* and *Homo habilis* were in existence some two million years ago, and, utilizing very primitive tools and weapons. For two million years little progress was made. And then, almost overnight, in terms of history, modern man was on the scene. Some twenty or twenty-five thousand years ago, Cro-Magnon man bust upon us with his advanced tools, his weapons, his religion, his advanced art."

"Advanced art?" Ronny protested.

"The cave drawings and paintings of the Magdalenian period in the Upper Paleolithic—especially in such places as Altamira in Spain and Lascaux in France—are not primitive art, as so many seem to think. It is a highly developed art, and, without doubt, connected with their religion. Consider a moment, and you will realize that the very concept of religion is indicative of a sophisticated mind."

Ronny said impatiently, "I don't seem to get the point."

"The point," the older man said reasonably, "is that possibly Cro-Magnon man was not native to Earth, but was either seeded there, or was the result of an ages-ago spaceship crash."

Ronny looked at him. "But there is no proof?"

"Not as yet. Perhaps one day it will be found on the Dawnworld planets."

"Dawnworld?" Ronny said. Then, "Never mind." He looked at Baron Wyler who had been leaning back in his chair, quiet but beaming encouragement. "What's this got to do with this preposterous idea that the, uh, Dawnmen aren't intelligent?"

The Baron said, "Count . . .?"

The elderly scholar ran a hand back through thinning hair, as though unhappy. "Your Excellency, are you at all acquainted with the caste system of early India?"

"No." Ronny hesitated. "That is, not much. I understand that it was one of the reasons India never got very far."

The academician looked at him unhappily. "Well, that is debatable. From your name and your facial characteristics, Your Excellency, I assume you are of European extraction. Europeans seem to have arrived at the opinion that their efforts have predominated in man's development. In actuality, few, if any, of man's really great breakthroughs originated in Europe. Indeed, the Europeans came late on the scene and were largely brought into the march of civilization despite themselves. This particularly applies to the Northern Europeans who are even more prone than others to think of themselves as the undisputed leaders."

The Baron's chuckle encouraged the old man.

He went on. "When my own Nordic and Tutonic ancestors were wearing animalskins and tearing their food from bones before campfires, the Indians were developing such advanced concepts as the zero, in mathematics. I mention in passing that the Mayans of Yucatan used the zero even before India. While my ancestors lived in skin-tents or inadequate shacks of wood and bark, large cities were being erected at Mohenjo-Daro and Harappa in the Indus River valley. Elsewhere in Asia and Africa, the wheel, the domestication of animals, agriculture, mathematics, astronomy—I could go on—were being developed. And my ancestors, and yours, Your Excellency . . ."

"And mine," the Baron laughed encouragingly.

". . . were still in their animalskins. Why, the art of writing has developed, in different form, in various places about the world: in China, in America, in Mesopotamia, in Egypt. The alphabet we use today had its origins in

Asia Minor. But to my knowledge, the Europeans had to import writing, never striking upon it on their own."

*The old boy was evidently capable of dwelling upon non-essentials indefinitely,* Ronny decided. "All right, all right," he said. "So the Indians made great strides, in spite of the caste system."

The scholar pursed his lips. "Or perhaps, because of it?"

"Oh, now, don't be ridiculous."

Count Fitzjames looked apprehensive, as though he feared he had gone too far.

But the Baron nodded to him. "Go on, my dear Count. Tell us a bit more of the caste system and its origins. And why you think it analogous to the Dawnworld's culture."

The other bobbed his head. "Yes, Your Lordship." He looked back at Ronny. "The origins of the system are lost in the mists of antiquity, but it is usually thought that when the Aryans invaded from the north—destroying the earlier culture, or assimilating it—they realized that unless they took stringent measures, they would soon interbreed and merge with the more numerous conquered indigenous people. So they divided society into four orders: the *Brahmins,* who performed religious and scholarly pursuits, the *Kshatriyas,* who were the ruling class and warriors, and the *Vaishyas,* traders and businessmen. All these were composed of the conquering Aryans. Intermarriage between castes was forbidden—a deep religious matter. Below these three castes were the *Sudras,* which were composed of the original peoples and took over the laboring jobs. Beneath these were the Outcastes, the untouchables, who were consigned to the most menial tasks.

"Now, consider. This system prevailed for a thousand years, two thousand years, or even more. A man born into the Brahmin caste became a scholar or religious; a Kshatryas, a soldier or ruler, and so on. A man born into one of the subdivisions of the Sudras was a cobbler, if his father, grandfather and so on had been. It never occurred to him to seek education, beyond what was involved in learning to make shoes. However, he did learn to make shoes and make them very well indeed. On the other hand, it never occurred to a Brahmin *not* to be educated. That was the nature of things. It was inevitable. Indeed, did he fail in his studies and application of them, as he had a good chance of being ostracized from society. What family would wish their perfectly normal, well-educated, Brahmin daughter to marry a cloddy? There were exceptions, of course, but on an average and over a period of time, the outstanding scholar in the caste got the pick of the girls. I assume your knowledge of genetics leads you the proper conclusions."

Ronny was looking at him thoughtfully. "I think I begin to see your ultimate point."

"Indeed. Actually, man on Earth has seldom come up with the type of socio-economic system that developed in India. Oh, there have been some. The so-called Incas of Peru were one. You were born into your social strata and could seldom, if ever, leave it. The Inca clan supplied the warrior-priests, the administrators; other clans supplied artisans; but most were of the soil and automatically became farmers." The old man looked up. "It worked, by the way, surprisingly well. The average inhabitant of Peru, at the time of the conquistadores lived on a considerably higher level than did the average inhabitant of Europe."

"The anthill," Ronny said, an edge of distaste in his voice.

The Baron shrugged and smiled pleasantly. "Perhaps," he said. "We are not exactly advocating such a socio-economic system, my dear Bronston; however, it has its admitted advantages."

"From your ambitious viewpoint."

"Granted. But the point the good Count is making is that man can evolve along such a path. He need not automatically follow the more individualistic road we most often witnessed in Earth's early development. On the Dawnworlds, it would seem—if we interpret the information we've accumulated correctly—they have taken a path of specialization unknown even in caste system India."

"But what has this got to do with your claim that they aren't intelligent?"

"My dear Bronston, extrapolate a bit on the example the good Count gave you of the cobbler. Suppose that instead of being a cobbler for two millennia, he stuck to his specialty for a megayear or so. No need for education, no need for anything—except learning to make shoes."

"Yes, but such a cloddy doesn't invent a method of converting matter."

"Are you sure? Our cobbler doesn't invent a matter converter, obviously. His field is shoes. But as the centuries go by, and the millennia, a slight improvement in technique here, a slightly different tool put into use there, and you'd wind up with some very nearly perfect shoes.

Remember, by this time he *instinctively* makes shoes. Over the megayears, the inadequate shoemakers, the throwbacks, have been weeded out. It has become a matter of genetics. The child born into the cobbler—let's call it caste—can make shoes without training. In the same manner that the bee takes no training to collect honey, nor the soldier ant to guard the community."

"But the matter converter?"

"Obviously devised by some other caste. Some caste which has been at work in manufacture a megayear or so. Undoubtedly, a member of this caste is no more capable of making shoes, other than putting them into a converter and copying them, than the cobbler is capable of producing matter converters, or fusion reactors."

The Baron pursed his lips. "Actually, of course, I doubt if they have cobblers at this late date. With the matter converter, such as skills would disappear."

He looked suddenly at the elderly scholar, "That will be all, Count Fitzjames."

The Count scrambled hurriedly to his feet, put his hand over his heart in the salute he had made when he entered the room, and backed hurriedly toward the door through which he had come half an hour earlier.

When he was gone, the Baron looked at his visitor. "It's all rather mind shaking, isn't it?"

Ronny didn't immediately answer. Finally, he shook his head, as though to clear it, and said, "Frankly, I can't understand your reason for letting me in on all this. Surely, you must realize I'll simply report to Ross Metaxa."

"I hope not," the Baron said seriously, pouring the remainder of the light wine into their glasses.

*All right, you've got it.* Ronny thought. *Start bouncing.*

The Baron said judiciously, "Largely, what your commissioner reported to the chiefs of state, there at the conference in the Octagon, is valid. Man is face to face with his greatest crisis. Nothing can prevent our coming in contact with the Dawnworlds and their unique culture, sooner or later. Probably sooner than we would wish. However, where Metaxa and I differ is in the manner in which United Planets must be organized most efficiently."

Ronny said, bitterly, "You, the strongman, figure on enforcing union."

The Baron smiled and sipped his wine. "My dear Bronston, has it never occurred to you that your admired Ross Metaxa is a strongman himself?"

"He works within the framework of the United Planets Charter."

The other clucked deprecation. "Does he, indeed? I am afraid, only when it so suits him. His methods differ little from my own, in actuality. He is downright Machiavellian when he can achieve his purpose by no other means. For instance, in selecting his tools . . . his agents, such as yourself. I am sometimes surprised that young men of obvious integrity and idealism, remain on his, ah, team."

Ronny could see something was coming. Another curve ball.

Baron Wyler said decisively, his friendly eyes boring earnestly into the Section G operative's, "Bronston, we of Phrygia know the location of the nearest Dawnworlds. We are on the verge of sending an expedition there. We are of the opinion that it will be quite practical to land and observe sufficient of that culture to be able to duplicate some of their ultra-advanced devices." He twisted his mouth. "If not duplicate them, perhaps, ah, liberate one or two. It would seem that the matter converter is highly portable, for instance.

"I hardly need point out that the possession of such a device would put our planet into such a position of advantage that the whole of United Planets, even if they could be coerced into acting in full unison, could not stand against us."

The Baron came to his feet, and his personality seemed to fill the room to straining. "Reunited under the aegis of Phrygia, man, of all the three thousand worlds we have colonized, will march forward together. By the time the inevitable all-out contact between the Dawnworlds and our own is made, we shall be ready for these unintelligent—though highly advanced technically—antmen, beemen, call them what you will."

Ronny looked up at him, expressionlessly. "And where do I come in on this? Why have you told me about it? Why do you hope I won't report to Ross Metaxa?"

Baron Wyler smiled at him. "I would think that as sharp a man as yourself, my dear Bronston, would see what I have been leading to. I am as desirous of top operatives as is Ross Metaxa. I want you to join my forces, Ronald Bronston."

Ronny looked at him.

He came to his own feet. "I see. You want a man planted in Section G who'll keep you tipped off to the latest maneuvers of Ross Metaxa."

"Why mince words? Obviously."

The Section G agent's mouth worked. He said finally, "I'll have to think about it. Frankly, what's been said here in the past hour has set me back on my mental heels."

"Of course, my dear Bronston. Do not take too long, is all. Events are on the march. We must not be dullards."

He made his way over to the wall screen he had utilized earlier, and said something into it.

The same door, through which the elderly Count Fitzjames had come, opened again and Rita Daniels entered the room.

86

Ronny stared.

She said, a mocking quality in her voice, "Good afternoon, Citizen Bronston." He had noted the comparative drabness of the local women on the streets, here was the direct opposite. Not even in the most swank salons, in the most luxurious embassies in Great Washington, could he have found a more stunningly turned out young woman than this. No Tri-Di star could have equaled this slim blonde; no artificially manufactured sex symbol, the pert prettiness of this elfin girl.

The Baron beamed at the two of them "I understand you have already met my niece, Your Excellency."

Ronny Bronston closed his eyes in pain.

Rita said sweetly, "This was quite a little gimmick, getting yourself appointed a plenipotentiary from UP. Or do you maintain that you bore that rank before reaching Phrygia?"

Ronny bowed, wryly. "You seem to have a gimmick or so up your own sleeve, Citizeness Daniels," he said.

The Baron smiled his wide smile. "Whatever our friend's immediate methods, my dear Rita, he obviously can think on his feet, a desirable trait." He turned to Ronny. "My niece has been working, ah, incognito, with Interplanetary News, the better to learn the workings of our fellow worlds. However, I believe I shall, in the future, utilize her talents even more profitably. Had I known what Metaxa had up his sleeve, I would never have allowed her to try and penetrate that conference; I had no idea he would go to the extent of seizing and then memorywashing the poor girl."

He turned back to Rita, "And now, my dear, will you see our guest to his quarters? He has some important decisions to make."

## IX

Rita took him up, by way of the private elevator, to the ground floor and through the pseudo-Minoan Palace to a hovercar ramp. As they progressed, silently, passers-by came to a quick halt. Civilians pressed their hands over their hearts in the same salute Count Fitzjames had given the Baron, soldiers came to stiff attention.

She looked at him from the side of her eyes, a mocking quality still there.

Ronny said dryly, "Like magic, isn't it? On Mother Earth, a lowly Interplanetary News reporter, sneaking into places she's not wanted. Being grabbed, manhandled, mauled, battered around, and then memorywashed. But now a veritable princess, the niece of the Supreme Commandant."

"What! Manhandled, mauled, battered around! Who dared?"

He looked at her as though in surprise. "Oh. That's right, you wouldn't remember."

She had stopped. Now she stood there, fists on boyishly slim hips, glaring at him. "You . . . you . . ." Then she caught his grin.

"Ha!" she snapped. "The last time you told me I had a bottle of guzzle, was drenched, and in trouble with a traffic coordinator."

He continued to grin, the mockery was in his face now.

She spun and marched on. "Someday, I'm going to find out what happened to me during that twenty-four hours," she snarled. "And when I do . . ."

They reached a wide entryway which led off toward the gates down the ramp. Rita snapped something to one of the guards, who then spoke into a screen set in the wall. In moments, a low slung auto-car approached them. It was a two seater, and Rita slid under the controls. She dropped the manual lever and took the stick, waiting for him.

Ronny got in beside her and they started down the ramp. He said, "I've got an official car waiting for me at the main gate."

"Let them follow. I want to talk to you."

"All right. My suite's at the United Planets Building."

When they passed the UP limousine with the marines, he gestured to them to follow.

Rita said, "What did you think of Uncle Max?"

"Uncle Max? Oh, the Baron."

"Maximilian, and a whole lot of other names and titles."

Ronny said warily, looking out over the countryside, "He surprised me." This whole area had been landscaped, all the way to the city. Phrygia evidently spared no expense in aggrandizing her Supreme Commandant.

She said, conversationally, "Have you ever noticed the extent to which man can delude himself when considering persons of whom he doesn't approve?"

"Such as strongmen?" he said dryly.

"Exactly. Evidently, few consider that men such as Alexander didn't stand alone. Actually, he was the leader of a team. A team of military and political geniuses so capable that they were able to pull down the world's greatest empire. Men like Parmenion, Ptolemy, Antipater, Antigonus, Seleucus and all the Companions. Can you see the charm he must have radiated, the strength, the ability to draw men of great capability into his serv-

89

ice? He must have indeed been like a god. Or Napoleon. Can you imagine the personality that man must have had, the charm, to draw together his team? Men like Ney, Marat, Bernadotte, Lannes, Soult and Masséna."

She shook her head so that the ponytail she affected flounced back and forth. "No, Ronny Bronston, your strongmen of history weren't dark villains with a mean glint in eye and dastardly deeds in mind. They were men of exceeding charm and strength, and they became strongmen because of the superiority."

"How does Hitler fit into this theory?" Ronny said mildly.

"He's come down to us as the archvillain of all time. And I have no doubt that his victims saw him in that light. But his immediate team evidently worshipped him. Even men of the caliber of Churchill admitted his personal charm, his strength of personality. Without it, he would never have swayed the people as he did."

They were proceeding toward the capital city at full tilt now, the marines in the car behind having their work cut out trying to keep up with the speedy two seater the girl drove.

Ronny looked over at her, not failing to note the spray of freckles dusted over her slightly upturned nose. "You seem to have read up quite a bit on history, especially the history of strongmen." He paused, before adding, "Could it be because you see another strongman, Uncle Max, coming along?"

"Obviously, Ronny Bronston. And I want to be part of his team. Don't you?"

Ronny said, "I thought I'd think about it a bit. I don't change coats as easily as all that."

She slowed the car's pace a trifle and put a hand on his sleeve. She said, an element of inspiration in her voice, "Of course you don't. But man has come as far as he can, Ronny, along the path as it is now. We *need* a strongman. What a glorious race we could become, if under the banner of Maximilian Wyler, we united to march together into the future."

"What future?"

"Eventually, the complete domination of the galaxy, no matter what other life forms we run into as we progress."

"That's quite an order," Ronny said mildly.

"Don't be silly. I don't mean within our lifetimes. But only that can be the eventual destiny of man."

Ronny said, "Suppose I granted that the race could use a strongman along here, a man on horseback, as the term goes. What leads you to believe that Uncle Max is the man?"

She frowned at him. "But isn't that obvious? If he isn't, he'll never form his team, he'll never come to power. History is strewn with the wrecks of would-be strongmen, who didn't really have what was required."

He nodded agreement. "You're right, there. If Baron Wyler isn't the man he thinks himself, he'll land on the rocks, too."

She drew up before the UP Building and brought the vehicle to a halt, although without setting it down. Her hand was on his arm again.

"Think it over, Ronny. My uncle evidently wants you on his team."

"All right," he said. "I'm thinking. Thanks for the ride."

He turned and taking two levels at a time, started up the stone steps. He didn't turn when he heard her sporter whisk away from the curb.

In the small apartment which had been assigned him,

he immediately went to his bag. He brought forth a small object looking something like a woman's compact or a cigar case. He sat down at the table and propped it before him, activating it.

"Phil Birdman," he clipped out. "Soonest."

Birdman's mahogany face faded into the miniature screen. "I've been waiting for you to call."

"Get over here," Ronny rapped. "I'm at the UP."

"Right." The Indian's face faded.

Ronny said, "Irene Kasansky. Soonest."

Irene's perpetually harrassed face faded in, and twisted into her version of a smile, when she saw who it was. "Hi, Ronny, what's the urgency?"

"I've got to talk to the Old Man, immediately."

"No can do. Another big conference. He's browbeating fifty or more presidents, kings, patriarchs and what not."

"Give me Sid, then. And let the chief know I have to talk to him."

"All right, but Supervisor Jakes is busy, too."

Sid Jakes faded in, grin wreathed as usual. "Ronny! Plenipotentiary Extraordinary! Frankly, in spite of that imposing tag, I thought the Baron'd have you into his deepest dungeon by now."

"Knock it!" Ronny clipped. "This is highest emergency. Everybody, but everybody, has been underestimating Uncle Max."

Sid Jakes' eyes widened slightly and his grin was a bit less bright. Not even in the seemingly lax Section G did an agent customarily tell Ross Metaxa's right-hand man to shut up.

"Who?" he asked.

Ronny briefed him on what had transpired.

The feisty Section G supervisor ran a hand over his mouth thoughtfully. "Hmmm, I wonder how it'd work out if you told the Baron you're signing up with him? Then we'd have you on the inside of his organization."

Ronny said plaintively, "I keep telling you, this Wyler is no cloddy. The moment I told him that, he'd slip me some Scop, just to see if I was lying. Then, when he found out my passion for him and his ambitions wasn't exactly overwhelming, he'd see I had a few holes blasted in me."

Sid said, "Yeah. Possibly, we'd better pull you out of there, Ronny. When you turn him down, the Baron isn't going to be very happy about the fact that he's revealed so much to you."

"You can't pull me out," Ronny said. "There's nobody else here but Phil Birdman, and the Baron is about to send his expedition to the Dawnworlds. If it succeeds, and he gets some of those ultra-ultra devices the Dawnmen have, the fat's really in the fire. That matter converter. If I get a clear picture, with it he could duplicate himself a fleet of space cruisers that would outnumber everything UP has combined."

"You have no idea where these Dawnworlds—where in Zen did that name ever come from?—are located?"

"None at all. The Baron learned through some of the things his people found on the little aliens' planets."

Jakes muttered, for once unsmiling, "Without coordinates, it could take us a millenium looking." He looked up again. "Listen, I'll get to Ross. Call you back."

While he had been talking, Phil Birdman had entered the room. Ronny deactivated the Section G communicator and turned to his colleague.

The Indian said, "Well, at least, you're still with us."

"But how long that will be, I couldn't guarantee," Ronny told him.

The older agent sank into an auto-chair and dialed.

"Pseudo-whiskey?" he asked. "I have a sneaking suspicion I'm going to need a bit of firewater before I've heard all your story."

They'd got through two highballs apiece before Ronny had finished bringing him up to date.

When he had ended, Birdman grunted. "There's only one answer," he submitted.

"What?"

"Let's go down to the recruiting station and join up with Uncle Max."

"Oh great, you overgrown funker. Funnies, I get."

The communicator hummed. Ronny went over to the desk, sat down before it and activated the device. It was Ross Metaxa, at least as rumpled and weary as usual. He minced no words.

"That madman is taking a gamble, in his bid for power, that could destroy us all. Our big chance was to put off for as long as possible first contact with these aliens. To stall for time. Now he's planning to set down on one of their planets, right now—to make immediate contact. He's drivel-happy! Well, there's nothing for it. Ronny, find out where these damned Dawnworlds are located."

"Yes, sir. How?"

"How in the devil would I know? You and Agent Birdman are there. I'm not. The nearest other agents to Phrygia are a good week's trip away. It's all in your lap."

Ronny Bronston looked at him.

His ultimate superior looked back, his eyes level.

On an impulse, Ronny blurted, "Was my becoming a Section G agent an engineered deal, not of my own choosing?"

The moist eyes looked deeply into his own, without flicker. "Yes."

Ronny took a deep breath.

Ross Metaxa said, "Report through Irene as soon as you have anything." His face faded.

Ronny turned to Phil Birdman, who had come up behind him to listen in on the conversation, but had missed even the final sentences. "You better dial us another drink, Phil. We're going to need it."

Phil, his expression passive, got the drinks, then sat down across from Ronny Bronston.

Ronny said slowly, "Phil, the Baron's working on a full time basis on this project. That means somewhere, on or very near his person, is the information we need—the location of the Dawnworlds."

The Indian said nothing.

Ronny said slowly, "Phil, the Baron isn't quite as well informed on Section G as he'd like to think he is. There're a few little items that come out of the gimmick department that—I'm willing to bet my life—he hasn't heard about."

Phil Birdman put down his glass.

Ronny said, "Phil, one of us has got to go in."

"You mean . . ." The older man ran his tongue over suddenly dry lips. He said, his tone a blend of protest and apology, "I'm forty-five, Ronny. There aren't many of the good years left."

"Metaxa would undoubtedly retire you immediately, on full pay, of course."

The other said slowly, "I don't want to retire. I like this work. Some day I look forward to making supervisor."

Ronny said, "All right. I'm only thirty-two."

Birdman looked up at him, his handsome Indian face working. "It's fifteen years off your life, Ronny."

Ronny Bronston nodded, a weary aspect in the gesture. "When I joined up with Section G, I figured I was expendable. This isn't as bad as copping a slug from some secret police goon on some backward planet, where we're trying to upgrade their government, or some such."

He thought of something and said, "By the way, Phil. How'd you get into Section G? What led you to apply?"

"Oh, I didn't. Sid Jakes looked me up one day while I was still living back on Piegan. I was in the local police. We jawed around a little and before I knew it, I was in."

"Kind of got jockeyed in, eh?" Ronny said bitterly.

Phil looked at him. "I wouldn't put it that way."

Ronny got up and went over to the order box on the desk. He said into it, "I want the biggest whale of a meal you can concoct. Very concentrated, rich food, high calorie content."

Later, they retraced the route the marines had driven him earlier in the day. Phil Birdman was driving now, his own speedy hovercar.

Ronny was pensive. He said, after a long silence. "How close do you figure we can get? That's important. It'll cut time."

Phil said thoughtfully, "On that diagram you drew: You know that ramp this Rita Daniels mopsy took you to, when you were leaving the palace?"

"Yes, sure."

"I can take you to the top of that."

"I think that's the private entry of the Supreme Commandant and his family."

"I know. As soon as I get to the top, they'll order me to drive down again. That's perfect for us. Every split second can count, Ronny. It could be seventeen or eighteen years, you know. . . ."

Ronny Bronston said nothing. For that matter, it had

been known to be twenty. Beyond that point, you inevitably died. You starved to death.

The hovercar bore diplomatic indentification. The guards did no more than present their spears in a salute as they roared through the palace gates. Phil Birdman kept up a good speed. Not so high as to be conspicuous, but fast enough that their faces were unlikely to be spotted.

They got to the foot of the ramp and started up.

"You'd better take it," the Indian said tightly, from the side of his mouth.

Ronny took a syrette from a small compartment in the dash and pushed it home in the back of his neck. He reached immediately for some of the energy pills.

Things were jerking frantically by the time they reached the head of the ramp and the entrada there—jerking frantically and already beginning to slow up.

A guard officer moved sluggishly toward them, more sluggish still. As he approached the car, his mouth, slowly, slowly, began to open. But before sound issued forth, he had stopped completely, one foot held in the air, his body in such position that it seemed impossible for him not to fall forward, out of balance.

Ronny Bronston vaulted over the side of the car and darted into the interior. He had done this but once before, in training, and had been under for less than ten seconds, pseudo-time. But this was the real thing. He darted a hand into his jacket pocket and gulped down more pep pills.

All was frozen.

He had no time to waste observing the utterly fantastic phenomenon. *The world had stopped.*

# X

He retraced the route Rita Daniels had brought him along only a few hours earlier, dodging around the frozen statues that had—moments before—been soldiers and officials, clerks and secretaries, in all their bustling activities.

He came to the private elevator that led into the depths that housed the apartments of the Supreme Commandant. This was his first serious barrier. There was no manner in which he could operate the machinery, nor any other machine, save the equipment he carried.

He whipped out a laser gun, flicked the stud to cut and began beaming a hole through the elevator shaft door. Pure luck was involved now. He grabbed the door handle, and when he had largely cut the door away, pulled it toward him. It was a fantastically thick door. Evidently, Phrygia security took care that it was not easy to get at their Supreme Commandant.

Finally, the door began to fall toward him, slowly, sluggishly, but sped up by the effort he was exerting. It was as though he were pulling it through water, or even a thicker fluid. Before it had half reached the floor, he gave up his efforts and peered into the shaft beyond.

Luck was with him. Built into the metal wall of the shaft were ladder steps, obviously meant for repairmen, and possibly as a last method of emergency exit from the quarters below in case of some extreme disaster.

He vaulted over the falling door, now arrested in its drop, and scurried down the ladder.

Ronny tried to remember how long it had taken him to get down to the Baron's apartments, when he had been there before, and couldn't. This was the crucial thing. If the other maintained his rooms five or ten stories down, that was one thing. If they were a hundred stories, that was disaster. He would starve to death in this shaft.

Which brought his needs to mind. He darted a hand into one of his pockets for another handful of energy pills, even as he descended.

Luck was with him still.

His feet hit the top of the elevator cab.

He pulled the gun again, even as he gobbled pep pills, and cut a hole through the top of the elevator cage. He jumped on the circular, cut away a section so that it would fall. As soon as it had fallen sufficiently for him to jump off onto the elevator cage floor, he did so, and turned the gun to the door, cutting that away, too.

Ronny pushed hard against the great inertia, forcing the door inward into the room beyond. He wedged himself through as soon as there was sufficient way.

He was within the Baron's apartments. Now he needed fortune's kiss, indeed. Suppose the Baron wasn't here. Suppose, even though he was, he didn't have the information on him. Suppose he did have it, but in such form that it was impossible to decipher.

Suppose a lot of things.

He darted his hand into another pocket for a supply of the energy pills, and dashed into the room in which Wyler had invited him earlier in the day. It was unoccupied.

He headed for the door beyond, through which both Count Fitzjames and Rita had entered. Happily, it was open. He sped down the hall that was there, searching

frantically. The living quarters of the Supreme Commandant of Phrygia were laid out in similar fashion—though
utterly more swank—to any home of an extremely wealthy
individual on a score of planets Ronny had visited. He
had little trouble in guessing the layout.

From time to time, he would pass frozen statues in
this dead world. Servants, guards, what were obviously
secretaries or clerks, sometimes, if garb meant anything,
evidently some high ranking Phrygia official.

*Somewhere along here*, Ronny thought, *must be some
sort of audience chamber, some sort of conference
room.* It was unlikely that Baron Wyler would be eating
at this time of day, and certainly not sleeping. Ronny
was gambling on the possibility that Wyler was at work,
in conference with underlings, and probably deep in the
project for sending the expedition to the Dawnworlds.

The gamble paid off.

He came to a large door guarded by two huskies in
elaborate uniform, muffle-guns at their sides.

He wrenched at the doorknob, miscalculated and
ripped it completely off.

Ronny snarled an obscenity, stepped back and flicked
his beam gun up again. He repeated the process of cutting a circular hole large enough to pass his body, and
then pushed the panel through. When there was space to
see, he realized he had found what he sought. The Baron
Wyler, standing at a table, a dozen men, mostly uniformed, also about it.

He pushed harder on the slowly falling panel, finally
had the space to squeeze through. The Baron was standing, mouth closed, looking down the arch of his aristocratic nose at one of his subordinates who was speaking,
his finger touching a chart. At least, he had been speaking at the moment of the freeze—his mouth was open.

And remained so, though no sound issued forth during Ronny's stay.

Ronny Bronston darted to the table. He stared down at the paper the other was touching. It was a star chart, but not, he realized, the one that could possibly have helped in the location of the Dawnworlds. It was a chart of United Planets.

Ronny sorted through the papers on the table, frantically. On the face of it, these men were discussing the broad subject of the Baron's designs against UP. If so, the subject of the Dawnworlds was obviously in mind.

But there was no other chart. Plans, reports, graphs, diagrams of this, that and the other. But no further charts.

He stepped over to the frozen statue that was Baron Wyler and ran his hands over him. He went through every pocket, examined, however briefly, every paper. The other's body felt like clammy clay, there was a nauseating element in making physical contact with a living object under these conditions.

There was nothing pertaining to the Dawnworlds.

For the briefest of moments, he wondered if it were all a hoax. Was the wily Baron planting the idea that he was in contact with this fabulous unintelligent race with the idea of bluffing the UP into accepting him as supreme? But no, the bluff might work with some, but hardly with others. Such planets as Delos were going to have to be shown something tangible before knuckling under to a Baron Maximilian Wyler.

Ronny Bronston's eyes began to dart around the room, inspecting the Baron's underlings. Which, of them all, might be expected to carry a star chart, pinpointing the Dawnman worlds? He simply didn't have time to search them all. The only one he recognized was the self-effacing Count Fitzjames, who, characteristically, was back away from the others, as though not wishing to intrude.

He grabbed energy pills from his jacket and munched on them. He had to think. No matter how desperate for time, he had to think.

He had been in this room already so long that he could note a slight change in the Baron's eyes. They had begun to widen a merest trifle, the first indication of surprise.

Then, as though magnet drawn, the Section G agent's attention whipped back to Count Fitzjames. What was the other doing over there, away from the others? Something hadn't at first registered on Ronny's awareness.

Yes! The oldster was looking at a . . . a map. No! It was a chart, a star chart. Ronny whipped over. Attached there to the wall.

Phrygia was heavily marked, down in this corner. Over here, surprisingly near, were the three star systems of the originally discovered tiny aliens. And beyond, all those numberless stars in red! They could only be . . .

Whether or not he was right, Ronny had no more time. No more time. He reached out and ripped the chart from the wall. Swore at himself for tearing it badly. Carefully and slowly pulled it down, folding it, so he could carry it more easily.

He spun and dashed for the door he had blasted through, slowed somewhat by the resistance of the object he carried. He wedged himself into the corridor beyond. The panel he had cut out had not as yet dropped all the way to the floor; in fact, was not more than an inch or so lower than when he had finished shoving it.

In the corridor, the guards were beginning to react somewhat as had the Baron. Their eyes had begun to widen in shocked surprise.

He hurried down the hall, retracing his steps. To the

elevator. Through the roof of the cage, up the ladder. As he went he desperately swallowed his energy pills, desperately crammed them down.

The ground floor could be no more than a few stories up, but he felt himself tiring. He was weary with the activity. He had been moving at top speed since Phil had pulled the hovercar up before the entry. And he could feel it now.

At least, that is what he told himself he was feeling.

He refused the fear that was welling up inside. How long, how long?

He pulled himself at last through the hole he had burned in the heavy elevator door at the ground floor. He began to drag himself along the way to the entry, the ramp, Phil's hovercar and release. The star chart he carried grew increasingly sluggish, impossibly heavy.

And even as he went, he knew he wasn't going to make it.

The energy was draining out of him with every step. He had taken too much time. He had taken far too much time.

He went down on his knees, the star chart falling slowly from his hands, then remaining suspended in the air. He laboriously took it again. He had to make it to the hovercar. He stumbled forward. It was far too far.

He was too weak even to bring more pep pills to his mouth. The last few he had taken had had little effect, at any rate. His body had taken all the punishment it was capable of taking. He wasn't going to make it.

This, then, was the ultimate failure.

He looked up in agony, down the long corridor that led to the direction of the ramp. The oocupants of the hall were still frozen in their movements. For him, they would always be frozen. But . . .

He saw movement!

Down the hall toward him came running Phil Birdman, his eyes going in all directions.

He spotted Ronny, grabbed down at him, hoisted him over his shoulder and started back.

Ronny held on to consciousness. He didn't understand, but it was going to work out now. He held desperately to the chart.

They were back in the hovercar. The Indian operative dumped him into the passenger seat, hurried around to the other side and vaulted into the driver's position. His hand darted to the dash compartment and seized two syrettes. He pressed the first into his own neck, the second into Ronny's.

Things began jerking frantically. Things began moving sluggishly. The people. The guards.

The guard officer, who had been walking toward them when time had first stopped, began moving more naturally, faster, and still faster.

Scowling, he barked, "What's going on here?"

Phil Birdman said apologetically, "Sorry, officer. I seem to have ascended the wrong ramp."

"You certainly have! This is the private entry of the Supreme Commandant! What's going on here? You men look suspicious."

The Phrygian stared at Ronny Bronston. "What've you got there in your hand? You didn't have anything just a second ago."

It was the star chart.

Ronny shook his head, weakly. "Nothing. I . . . I feel sick. Let's go on back, Birdman."

"Yes, get out of here," the guard officer rapped. He was scowling, obviously wondering whether or not to arrest this pair.

Phil Birdman had never dropped the lift lever. Now he applied pressure to the velocity pedal, tipped the stick to the left and back, and spun the vehicle to descend the ramp again.

Ronny fumbled for a sandwich, gobbled it. Got it down and felt like retching. There was a bottle with a score of assorted pills. He got them all down, drank deeply from a flask of water. He was dehydrated, weak, empty.

They were speeding toward the gate through which they had entered mere moments ago by straight time.

The gate was closing. The guards were milling about, anxiously. Four or five barred the way, spears raised.

Spears raised as though they were rifles, and it came to Ronny Bronston that appearances deceive. The Baron Wyler wasn't about to arm his guards with nothing more effective than iron tipped wooden shafts. Those spears were undoubtedly disguised weapons demanding of considerably more respect.

"Blast through!" Ronny clipped to his companion.

Phil shot a glance at him. "If I do, we'll have the paleface cavalry after us in moments."

"We've got them after us already. What d'ya think they're closing those gates for?"

The Indian's hand shot out, flicked a switch. Part of the dash fell away to reveal a pistol grip built into the car. Phil Birdman grabbed it, touched the trigger, slowly swerved the car right and left.

The gate and the soldiers that guarded it melted away into nothingness.

The two Section G agents felt nausea. It was seldom one took human life, even in the ultra-dedicated Bureau of Investigation.

They shot through what had once been the gate and down the road toward the city limits of Phrygia.

Ronny growled, "They'll be after us both in the air and on the road. Chances are, we'll never make it halfway."

"It's getting dark," Birdman muttered. "Not that that'll make much difference. You got the location of the Dawnman planets?"

"I think so." Ronny wolfed another sandwich. "Listen, how did you ever find me? What was the idea? How could you do it?"

Birdman grunted. "I pressed my syrette a split second after you did. I was gambling that my metabolism wouldn't be hit until you had already been gone long enough to do what you could. I figured that you'd probably keep going, long after you'd passed the danger point, if you hadn't found what we needed. I figured I'd be going into pseudo-time, just in time to come looking for you."

He added apologetically, "It was all I could do. Of course, I was in pseudo-time only a fraction of the duration you were. I doubt if it makes more than a year or two difference."

"You cloddy!" Ronny growled. "Well, thanks." He knew well enough Phil would have kept coming, looking for him, no matter how much time had elapsed.

"All for dear old Section G," Phil said cheerfully. "Listen, I can hear them behind us. We'll never make it."

"Keep going," Ronny muttered. "I'm beginning to feel the immediate after-effects."

"Oh fine," the Indian operative said. "You haven't got a communicator on you?"

"No, of course not. We couldn't take the chance of the Baron getting hold of one of us and finding the thing. He'd be able to tap Section G communications."

106

The dash screen lit up. There was the face, the icy face of an officer in the uniform of Baron Wyler's personal guards.

The officer snarled, "You have exactly two minutes in which to come to a halt and surrender. Otherwise, we blast. You are not going to be allowed to reach Phrygia city limits. The Supreme Commandant's orders."

Ronny flicked the screen off. "Two minutes to go," he said. "Can you think of anything?"

"All I can think of," Phil said expressionlessly, "is that we should have taken my earlier idea. Go down to the recruiting station and join up with the Baron."

"To late now." Ronny grunted. "We've taken our stand. Look out, here comes a car toward us from the city."

"Probably a civilian," the Indian muttered. "There hasn't been time for security guards to be coming from that direction."

"Wait a minute!" Ronny said urgently. "I know that car. Stop."

The Indian shot a quick glance at him, but jammed on deceleration.

Ronny waved at Rita Daniels.

"Hey!" he called.

She came to a halt, her high forehead furrowed.

"What're you doing out there?" she asked. "I thought you were in town thinking over Uncle Max's proposition."

He was feeling increasingly weak, but he climbed from Birdman's hovercar and made his way to hers, fumbling as he went for his gimmicked fountain pen.

He said, "Look, I want to talk to you. Come along with us."

Her eyes narrowed. She could hear the sounds of the pursuing guard vehicles. "Not likely," she snapped. "What're you up to?"

He lifted the stud of the device and turned to call weakly to Birdman. "Get the Baron on the screen. Soonest, damn it!"

He turned back to the girl. She was scratching her cheek where the tiny dart had struck her, and already her eyes were going blank.

"Come along with me, Rita," he ordered. Without bothering to see if she followed, he staggered back to the other hovercar.

Phil Birdman had managed to get through. Evidently, Baron Wyler had been stationed at a screen wating for a report from his guards on the progress of the chase. His face was on the screen.

Ronny Bronston slumped into his seat, the drugged girl climbed in next to him, the slim figure warm but unnoticed against his side.

He said weakly, "We've got your niece, Uncle Max. She's going with us into Phrygia."

The Baron's face was blazing with anger. "Have you supposed altruists of Section G stooped to abducting helpless women and using them as hostages to protect your miserable selves?"

"You have said it, friend," Phil Birdman said flatly. He kicked the acceleration pedal with his foot, switched off the screen again to prevent the other from following their conversation.

Ronny Bronston had been hanging on to consciousness with considerable effort. Now he gave up.

## XI

Ronny came to, weakly, in the hideaway the Indian operative had made in the suburban housing area of the Phrygian capital. Evidently, Phil had just given him a draught of something highly stimulating.

"How'd you ever make it?" Ronny murmured.

Phil grinned down at him. Bronston was stretched out on a couch. "Ugh. Redman have no trouble shaking pursuing palefaces in confusion of big city traffic."

"Funnies, I get," Ronny muttered. "Where's the girl?"

"She's with us. Our strongman isn't as strong as he ought to be, if he's thinking in terms of taking over whole empires of planets. He should have figured her expendable."

Ronny said, before passing out again, "Get the Old Man."

Phil Birdman went over to the desk and set up the Section G communicator. He said into it, "Irene Kasansky, soonest."

Her tight face faded in, her expression worried. "Phil Birdman," she said, "what's going on?"

"Give me the Chief, Irene. Absolutely soonest."

"He and Jakes are waiting for your report."

Metaxa's acid sour face faded in. "Birdman!" he growled. "What's happened to Ronny Bronston?"

The Indian said, "I've got him here. He's out." He had an edge of bitterness in his voice now. "He took your orders literally, of course. The only way of getting that information was for him to go into pseudo-time."

Ross Metaxa stared at him, unblinkingly. "How long was he under?"

"Evidently maximum. He probably set some sort of record."

The Section G head allowed himself to close his eyes for the briefest of seconds. He took a deep breath and said, "Did he get the information from that funker?"

"I think so. He brought a star chart away with him." Phil Birdman cleared his throat. "We also have a hostage. The Baron's niece."

Ross Metaxa assimilated that, not bothering to ask for details. He said, finally, "Have you any manner of getting out into space?"

Birdman hesitated. "UP has a small craft assigned to it. But if we utilize that, I have no doubt that the Baron will lower the boom on all UP personnel, the moment we're gone. He's got a reputation for ruthlessness, when he gets excited about something."

Metaxa shook his head. "They'll have to take their chances. You and Ronny and the girl get yourselves out. There's a Space Forces cruiser heading at top speed for you. They'll be there in five days, Earth time."

"Then what do we do?" Birdman said, though he could see it coming. "Return Ronny to Earth for whatever treatment he can get?"

Ross Metaxa looked at him bleakly. "The Baron is going to head immediately for those Dawnworlds. You take off after him. In a week's time, Bronston will have recovered."

The Indian said flatly, "Ronny Bronston will never recover, as you well know, Commissioner. He's lost at least twenty years in that jazzed up phoney-time he went into. Five years from now, he'll look and be twenty-five years older than he is today."

Metaxa said evenly, "He knew what he was doing, Birdman. He did what he had to do. He wouldn't have been Ronald Bronston otherwise. He'll recover within a week. As you know, the age doesn't come immediately, but over a period of time. For awhile, it won't effect him. When he has recovered, give him the story and make your way immediately after the Baron."

The Indian operative scowled. "How do you know the Baron, personally, will go out to the Dawnworlds?"

"Because when men like Maximilian Wyler really get in the clutch there's nobody they dare trust. He could never be certain that his closest right-hand man wouldn't take over the reins, given some of those gismos the Dawnmen evidently have. No, you can be sure that the Baron will go himself."

His face faded from the screen.

Birdman looked at the now opaque screen for a long moment. "So everybody's expendable, including the complete UP staff on Phrygia. The party's getting rough."

Ross Metaxa had been right. By the time the four man Space Forces cruiser reached them, Ronny Bronston was in his old shape. Good food and rest had done it. He felt the same as ever. All except, deep within, he knew that he had thrown away at least twenty years, the good years, of life. A few Earth years from now and he would look and be as old as Metaxa himself. It wasn't the happiest of prospects.

No effort whatsoever was being made to apprehend them. The Baron's regard for his niece evidently precluded any attempt by the Phrygian spaceforces to find and destroy their craft.

It occured to Ronny Bronston that if the girl were as close as all that to the would-be dictator, perhaps she had information about the man that might be of use in later developments. As he rested in the small space vessel that they had taken over from UP, he tried to pump her, though with precious little luck.

To the extent she could, in the confined space allotted to her nd the two Section G operatives, she tried to ignore them. From time to time, though, temper flared and she allowed herself to be drawn into argument.

The time, for instance, that she snapped out of a clear sky, "I don't see why you don't recognize that UP needs a leader such as Uncle Max."

Ronny said mildly, "Perhaps it does."

"Then why are you trying to hinder him? Why don't you join him?" she demanded.

Ronny looked at her wryly, "He hasn't proven to my satisfaction, as yet, that he's the man he thinks he is. Perhaps history will prove otherwise. As you pointed out the other day, it is strewn with the wreckage of would-be strongmen, who didn't make it."

"My uncle will make it!" The girl's natural attractiveness was accentuated in anger.

"Meanwhile"—Phil Birdman grinned at her—"there are a few of us who don't think so."

Ronny said, "Many aspire to supreme power, few are chosen. Take those examples you gave me the other day: Alexander, Napoleon, Hitler. They each supply a lesson.

"Alexander, for instance. He conquered the biggest empire known up to that time, but died at about my age from his inability to conquer himself. And when he died he left precious little. His immediate family, including his son, were killed off. That wonderful team of his fell apart, each trying to seize absolute power. Of them all, Ptolemy didn't do so badly; he and his descendants got

Egypt as their chunk of the pie. But the next fifty years and more was spent by the Macedonians trying to find another strongman, and failing"—Ronny twisted his mouth—"Their energies might have been put to better use.

"Or take your other example, Napoleon. He had his absolute power for awhile, but he was still in his forties when they kicked him out and he wound up his life there on St. Helena. And his team? They didn't do so well, either. Some turned traitor on him, when the bets were down. Some were shot. Of them all, Bernadotte, who became king of Sweden, was about the only one who came out ahead of the game.

"And Hitler . . ."

"Oh, he's the best lesson of all." Phil laughed. "That's the fella who taught me to believe in strongmen."

Rita Daniels was flushing, and on her it looked remarkably good, Ronny Bronston decided. However, something came to him and he brought himself up. As a man in his early thirties, he could consider a girl of Rita's age and weigh her in the balance as a potential life companion. But as a man past fifty, as he would be, all too soon, it wasn't in the cards. If Ronny Bronston were ever to consider marriage, he'd better steel himself to the fact that he had better begin looking at widows in their middle-forties, not frecklenosed girls in their twenties—no matter how provocative their ponytail hairdos.

Rita said snappishly, "The end of the strongman isn't always disaster. Ghengis Khan and Tamerlane founded dynasties. And though Alexander died a young man, and didn't leave one, still, it was through his efforts that Hellenism emerged and the Greek culture was spread from the Mediterranean to India. And Napoleon. When he stepped onto the scene, Europe was almost entirely feudalistic. When he left it, there was a new and more progressive socio-economic system."

Ronny continued to needle her. "Whether or not Hellenism was an advance over the Persian culture can be debated, my dear. The Greeks wrote the history books, since they won the war, but there are some doubts about just how progressive they were. If Hitler had won his war, you can be sure that the villains who came down to us would have been Churchill, Roosevelt and Stalin— not Adolph the Aryan, who would have been properly deified, as was Alexander before him."

Phil Birdman snorted and went over to check the control screens. "This waxes too intellectual for me," he complained. "I'm simple at heart. I just don't like guys in a position above me to make arbitrary decisions. Sometimes it hurts—me."

"Sometimes we need men with the ability to make quick, arbitrary decisions," Rita snapped.

"Yeah," Phil agreed over his shoulder. "But I like to be in a position to help decide who it's going to be. Any of these stutes with big ambitions will tell you they've got super abilities and you ought to let them make the decisions. But if those abilities of theirs aren't really so super, then I'm the cloddy who winds up crisp."

Ronny added mildly, "Our friend Hilter was a good example. He let the German people know he was the superman to end all. And they believed him."

"Oh, you're both flats!" Rita flared.

Ronny said, "Well, your Uncle Max is evidently making his play. I hope we're alive to see whether or not he succeeds."

Rita said scornfully, "If he makes it, my friend, I doubt if you'll survive long enough to enjoy the advantages of his guided political system." But even as she said it, her facial expression changed, and she looked at Ronny anxiously.

Phil, from the controls, laughed. "Touché. She's got you there, Ronny." He looked into a zoom-screen. "Hey, I think our Space Forces cruiser is coming in."

They considered, briefly, releasing the girl and allowing her to return to Phrygia in the small spacecraft they had taken over from the UP, which had been their home for the past week.

In fact, they called the UP Building with the intention of discussing her release, in return for leniency toward the United Planets personnel.

The only response was from a uniformed Phrygia security police colonel, who informed them coldly that there were no longer any UP personnel in the building and that he was not free to discuss the situation. He inquired after the health of their prisoner, but showed no emotion when he was told that it was excellent.

Phil Birdman looked at his colleague. "We'd better take her."

Ronny didn't like it, but he had no valid argument against continuing to keep an obviously valuable hostage. Whatever force the Baron had taken to the Dawnworld's with him, always assuming that their guess was correct and he actually was on his way, was most certainly more than this tiny space Cruiser with its crew of four.

He said unhappily, "There'll be six of us in that small ship as it is. She'd make it seven. Besides, who knows what trouble she might kick up? She's fanatically for her Uncle Max and might try to blow us all up, just on the off chance that it might help him."

115

Phil Birdman looked at him questioningly.

Ronny said, "We'd have to have her under guard for the whole trip."

Phil said reasonably, "Why not put her into cold for the duration? We can arouse her as soon as we want her awake. It won't hurt her."

Ronny said grudgingly, "I suppose we could do that."

The skipper and the three junior Space Forces officers of the little cruiser were taken aback by the fact that they were to have a feminine fellow passenger, and a pretty one. And not to speak of the fact that she was the kidnapped member of the royal family of Phrygia.

This particular vessel, the Space Cruiser *Pisa*, had been the nearest to Phrygia when the crisis arose. Ross Metaxa had thrown his weight around and quickly had the *Pisa* diverted to the trouble spot. The instructions were to put ship and crew at the service of the two Section G operatives. Captain Gary Volos and his three juniors hadn't the vaguest idea of what the assignment was to be.

Rita Daniels didn't help matters any.

At the first opportunity, and before Ronny could hardly more than begin his explanations to the Space Forces skipper, she had yelped, "I am being detained illegally. I am the Countess Rita Daniels Wyler, niece of the Supreme Commandant of the member planet Phrygia of the United Planets, and these criminals are violating Article One of the United Planets Charter. I demand to be returned to my uncle's palace on Phrygia immediately."

Captain Volos was shocked. His eyes went from her to the two Section G agents in disbelief.

"Some squaw," Birdman muttered.

Only then did it come to Ronny Bronston that he had been concentrating so long on the present emergency

116

that he had forgotten that not one person in a billion, in the overall population of the United Planets, knew that the emergency existed. The average member of the human race had no knowledge of the existence of the original little intelligent alien life form, not to speak of the Dawnworlds and the Dawnmen.

He rapped, "Captain, your orders are to place your ship and yourself and men under the command of Agent Birdman and myself. We'll hold you to that."

Volos, staring, retorted, "My superiors made no mention of my condoning the breaking of the United Planets Charter. Do you deny this citizeness' words?"

Ronny shook his head wearily. "Substantially, she is telling the truth. However, the circumstances are drastic."

"Drastic!" one of the junior officers retorted. "How can anything be so drastic that the UP Charter be violated? Why, that's the reason for the existence of the Space Forces. That's why I joined it. To preserve the United Planets Charter—with my life, if necessary."

"Oh fine," Phil muttered. "A flag waver. Just what we need."

"You're going to have your chance to die for United Planets," Ronny snapped back, impatiently. "This young lady's uncle is attempting to subvert it. Right now, he's on his way to some newly discovered planets with a type of man far in advance of the . . . well, the human race. He hopes to get ultra weapons and techniques that will enable him to take over complete control of every planet, United Planets members and otherwise, which our species has colonized. That's why you were sent out here: To help us stop him."

The four spacemen were staring at him as though he had gone completely around the bend.

Rita saw her opportunity. "See?" she demanded. "He's out of his mind."

"Obviously," the flag waver said, his eyes wide.

"Knock it, Richardson," his captain ordered. "I'll take care of this." He turned back to the two Section G agents. "I don't know what's going on here, but I'm going to land and check with the local delegation of United Planets."

"That'll be a neat trick, as Sid Jakes would say," Birdman muttered. "The local delegation of UP has either been shot or thrown into the cooler."

"I keep telling you," Ronny said, trying to maintain reasonableness in his tone, "Phrygia is in a condition of armed aggression against her fellow members of UP and in revolt against the UP as a whole."

"You mean to tell me," Captain Volos demanded unbelievingly, "that this planet wants to take on all three thousand worlds of the UP and conquer them?"

Rita laughed mockingly.

Ronny Bronston closed his eyes in pain. He opened them again.

He said, "Phil, cover them!"

A Model H gun flowed into Phil Birdman's hand.

## XII

"Captain," Ronny said mildly, "your orders are to put yourselves and your cruiser under the command of Agent Birdman and myself. We are going to insist you observe them."

The skipper's eyes went down to the gun. He recognized the competent manner in which it was being handled. He also recognized the weapon and its potentialities. He checked his three juniors with his eyes. Even Richardson avoided the question in his commanding officer's face.

Captain Volos said coldly, "I am acting under coercion, Citizen Bronston, and wish the fact to be entered into the *Pisa's* log."

"Very well. Within a short time, I'm going to prove to you what we've tried to put over. You don't seem to be a flat. When the proof is obvious, then Citizen Birdman and I will expect more hearty cooperation on the part of you and your men. Meanwhile, here is a chart. We are to head for the first of these sun systems marked in red."

The four hesitated for a long moment.

Birdman jiggled his gun, meaningfully.

The captain took the torn chart, scowled at it, took it over to his navigating table.

"Where'd you get this?" he asked grudgingly.

"It's a long story," Ronny told him. "Once we get underway, I'll tell you at least part of it. Suffice to say, for the moment, that I liberated it from our friends on Phrygia, who are trying to take over control of every human being alive."

The captain looked with continued disbelief at him, then turned down to the chart.

Phil Birdman said cheerfully, "I think we'd better chill the squaw here, like I suggested. She's already caused enough trouble in just these past few minutes. What could she accomplish working on our cloddy friends, here, over a period of a couple of Earth weeks, or so."

Rita looked at Ronny. "You plan to put me in cold?"

"Can you think of something better to do with you?"

"I refuse!"

He didn't bother to answer her.

"That's illegal!" one of the other junior officers said belligerently. "Illegal, without the permission of the subject."

The Indian laughed. "Friend," he said, "you're probably going to see one hell of a lot of illegality in the next few weeks, so you might as well start getting acclimated to it." He looked at Ronny. "You realize we're going to have to take this in shifts, don't you? We aren't going to be allowed to both sleep at once."

Ronny sighed and nodded. "Now let's see about this girl's shot."

The trip to the Dawnworlds went with little incident.

Ronny Bronston and Phil Birdman made no effort to interfere with ship routine and Captain Gary Volos' prerogatives. They conducted themselves as passengers with but one great difference.

They stood alternating eight hour watches. Never was there a time when both slept. Never was there a time when their weapons weren't immediately to hand.

They had taken measures, the first day, to put the

*Pisa's* small arms under lock, and remained the only men aboard with guns.

Largely, they spent their time playing battle chess with young Richardson, or with Mendlesohn or Takashi, the other two junior officers. The skipper himself refused to associate with the Section G agents beyond what was necessary to operate the spacecraft.

Ronny had thought he was making some progress with Richardson and Takashi, at least. Since they were going to be as exposed to the dangers of the Dawnworlds as anyone, he could see no reason for not giving the others all the information he held himself. This included a complete rundown on the true nature of United Planets and of Section G. It included the information about the little aliens, and the further information that this species had evidently been wiped out in their entirety by the Dawnmen.

He told them about the desperate efforts being made by Ross Metaxa and other ranking officials of the Octagon to bring complete unity to the United Planets, in order to prepare men for the eventuality of the touching of the two cultures. And he told them of Baron Wyler's ambitions and his present expedition to the Dawnworlds.

He had thought he had been making progress and was disillusioned the seventh Earth day after they had left the vicinity of Phrygia.

Phil Birdman had been playing battle chess with Mendlesohn, by far the best player aboard, which irritated the Indian since he rather fancied his own game. At this point, Birdman's double line of pawns were in full retreat before the other's strong armor attack. And Phil was muttering unhappily to himself, even as he tried to fight a delaying action until he could bring up his own heavier pieces.

Richardson, seemingly about nothing more important than crossing the small mess hall lounge for coffee, suddenly launched himself on the Section G agent's back.

Birdman, with no time to unholster his weapon, fell to the floor, the other clinging desperately to him, and tried to roll out. Mendlesohn, his eyes wide, scurried about the two threshing men as though not quite sure whether to throw his inconsiderable weight into the fray.

From the doorway, H gun in hand, Ronny snapped, "All right. Break it up. Richardson! On your feet, or I'll muffle you."

The aggressive ensign stood up, panting, his face unrepentant.

Phil Birdman sat there for a moment, shaking his head ruefully. "Why'd you stop it?" he growled at Ronny. "Now I'll never know if I could have clobbered the young yoke."

Ronny said, "You're too old to be rolling around on the deck."

"Huh," Birdman snorted, pushing himself erect. "Look who's talking. It won't be long before . . ." He cut himself short.

Ronny Bronston looked at him bleakly.

"Sorry," Phil said. "That's the trouble with wisecrackers. A supposedly smart quip gets out before you realize it's jetsam."

Ronny said to Richardson, "What was the idea?"

The other glowered resentment, in spite of the leveled gun. "What do you think it was? You've taken over the ship at gun point. I was trying to recapture it."

The captain entered from the compartment entrance opposite the one Ronny occupied. "What's going on?" he demanded.

"This cloddy here is making like a hero," Ronny said mildly. "I'm afraid we're going to have to ask you to put him in cold, Captain Volos."

"He's a necessary member of my crew!"

Phil Birdman muttered, "He's about as necessary as a coronary."

Ronny Bronston, still holding the gun, said, "So long as we're in underspace, you could handle the ship single-handed, Captain, as you well know."

"I refuse to put a man into cold without his permission."

Ensign Richardson glared defiantly at the Section G agent.

Ronny said mildly, "Then I'll have to shoot him. I can't afford to take the chance of having him loose. Next time, he might succeed."

"Not if he tried it on me," Birdman said nastily.

Ronny looked at Richardson, then the skipper. "The fat's in the fire, gentlemen. One man's life isn't very important."

Richardson said tightly, "Captain, I think he means it."

Captain Gary Volos rasped, "Very well, but I insist that this, too, be entered in the ship's log."

"That log is going to be plumb full before this trip's over." Birdman grinned.

Afterwards the two agents sat in the lounge alone over hot drinks.

Ronny growled, "It was lucky I couldn't sleep."

"Aw, I could've scalped that molly," the Indian grumbled.

"Not if Mendelsohn would have got around to slugging you on the back of the head."

Birdman chuckled. "Two down and only three left to go. You think we'll ever get there without putting them all in the cold? The party gets rougher and rougher."

Ronny asked suddenly, "Phil, why'd you join Section G?"

"Who, me?" Phil seemed embarrassed. "I don't know. Better job than I had. Chance to see a lot of the different planets. Get out of the rut. That sort of thing."

Ronny Bronston went on, as though he hadn't really heard his companion. "When I was a kid I had the United Planets dream but good. Man exploding out into space, carrying our species to the stars. Going every which way, trying every scheme ever dreamed up from Plato's Republic to Howard Scott's technocracy. Trying out every proposed ethic. Trying out a hundred methods of improving the race, by breeding in this, or breeding out that. Planets colonized by nothing but Negroes, others by only people over six and a half feet tall, others by Zen Buddhists, others by persons with I.Q.s of over one-fifty, others by vegetarians, and on and on."

Phil snorted, missing the earnestness in the other's tone. "How about Amazonia? A few thousand feminists. No men at all, at first. Artificial insemination. Then when boy kids came along, they enslaved them."

Ronny said impatiently, "Sure, a lot of them are purely from jetsam, but they're balanced out by those that are finding new paths, new truths, and really advancing the species. The United Planets dream. An opportunity for everybody to try anything. But what's the ultimate aim? What's the goal? To dominate the whole galaxy, the way Rita sees it?"

Phil looked at him questioningly. "Does there have to be a goal?" He was beginning to catch the other's mood.

"That's my point. I wonder if there should be. I wonder if the dream wasn't going better before the Octagon stepped in and decided that UP needed direction."

"Well, you know how the Old Man would answer that. It was fine to let mankind take off in all directions back when we had no reason to believe there was other intelligent life in the galaxy. But when we ran into those little fellows, then we had to get underway."

Ronny's expression was strange. "But underway where? A comparatively small group of men, of Ross Metaxa's type, decided it was up to them to steer. But of what are they composed that they should know best? Why should Ross Metaxa, and his various supervisors such as Sid Jakes and Lee Chang Chu, be allowed to decide that the government of this planet Amazonia, for instance, should be overthrown and a bi-sexual regime encouraged? Perhaps the matriarchy they're experimenting with is superior."

"Yeah." Phil grinned. "And perhaps not. Especially for *me*."

"Yes, but my point is, who is Metaxa to decide? There are tens of billions of members of the race. What makes him so special that he can throw Section G into a local situation on some planet colonized by this opinion group, or that, of their own free will and conscious of what they were going into?"

At long last, Phil Birdman turned thoughtful. "Maybe I don't know the answer," he admitted. "And maybe my decision was a wrong one. But I'm in my mid-forties now and I took my stand quite a time ago. I'm not going to change it now." He looked at Ronny. Are you?"

Ronny grunted self-deprecation. "I wouldn't know what to change it to."

Ronny Bronston came up behind Captain Volos, who

was standing watch in the *Pisa's* control compartment. He said, "What's wrong?"

The skipper was bug-eyeing into a zoom-screen. "A spacecraft! I've never seen another ship in underspace before. But . . . but that's not it. It's the size. It's as large as a medium-sized satellite."

Ronny said, "Let me see."

The captain grudgingly made room for him.

"I don't see anything," Ronny said.

The captain scowled at him and bent over the horizontal screen again. "It's gone!" he blurted. "It can't be gone!"

"We seem to be approaching the Dawnworlds," Ronny said dryly. "From what little I know about the Dawnmen, shortly, we're going to be witnessing a good many things that simply can't be."

Gary Volos was still gaping into the zoom-screen.

Ronny said, "How far out are we?"

The captain at last stood erect. "Not very far," he said. "I can't be too sure. I have no references except that chart you gave me. Possibly the coordinates are off. However, we should be coming out of underspace before long."

He looked at Ronny Bronston with puzzlement in his face, and also a touch of accusation. He said, "That craft I just saw was far and beyond anything that could be built on any United Planet's world."

Ronny said mildly, "I told you that the Dawnworlds are evidently fantastically beyond us, technically."

Volos shook his head. "I didn't believe your story. I didn't know what your game was, but I didn't believe this tale about other intelligent life forms."

"Well, Captain, you'd better start thinking about it.

The more cool minds we've got around, when we come out of underspace, the better off we're going to be. We have only one small bit of evidence that these critters won't crisp us immediately upon our materializing."

"What's that?" Volos asked, a shade of apprehension in his tone now.

"Those little aliens had photographs, both still and movies, on them. That would indicate that the little fellows actually landed on at least one of the Dawnworlds and were allowed to use whatever camera devices they had and then leave again."

He indicated the chart on the navigation table. "And that star chart. It shows hundreds of star systems in red. I've assumed that those are all Dawnman settled. The little fellas must have sent out various expeditions to compile that extensive a chart. Which means, in turn, that the Dawnmen allowed them to do it."

"Didn't you say that the atmosphere of the planets the little aliens were on was changed to what was poison for them?"

"That's right. Eventually, they must have done something to irritate these Dawnmen; but before they did, they must have done considerable exploring about the Dawnmen domains."

Ronny thought for a moment, then said, "I suppose you might as well start the process of reviving Rita Daniels and young Richardson. We're not going to be in any position to remain divided among ouselves after breakout from underspace."

"All right," the captain said nervously. He spoke into an order box.

Ronny said, "Look. This trip hasn't been any too happy, thus far, which isn't surprising. But now that we're here,

I want to let you know that so far as the operation of the *Pisa* is concerned, Agent Birdman and I want to cooperate. You're the captain. We'll follow orders."

Volos looked shamefaced. "My instructions were to put myself and command under your orders. I'm sorry I got around to following them so tardily. Very well. I captain the *Pisa*, but the overall decisions are yours."

His eyes flicked to the control panels. "We're coming out." He reached over and threw an alarm.

Within moments, Birdman and Lieutenant Takashi hurried into the compartment.

Takashi, his characteristically bland face showing unoriental-like excitement, said, "Mendlesohn's bringing the others out of the cold."

The captain said, "We're emerging."

They came out in the planetary system of a sun remarkably like Sol, and within reasonable distance of a planet most remarkably similar to Earth.

The captain muttered, "The coordinates were as perfect as any I've ever seen. Much better, in fact."

Phil Birdman said, "We told you, those little aliens were far and gone in advance of us. Evidently in interplanetary navigation as well as elsewhere."

Rita Daniels and Ensign Richardson, both looking a bit green about the gills, came into the compartment, cups of some steaming broth in hand.

The captain, his eyes magnetized to the large screen which took up a full half of one control compartment wall, threw a lever. Richardson put down his cup and slid into a control chair, so did Takashi.

The captain said to Ronny Bronston, "Well?"

Ronny shrugged. "Why put it off? Let's go closer." He had an afterthought and said, "You people have some method of detecting any craft down below using nuclear propulsion, haven't you?"

"Of course. It's part of the equipment utilized to locate possible wrecks of spacecraft, which have crashed."

"Could you locate the Baron's ship, or fleet, as the case may be?"

Volos frowned. "Why do you think he's here? There are hundreds of star systems on that chart."

"I'm not sure he is," Ronny told him. "But this is the nearest of them all. Why should he go further, if he's in a hurry?"

Rita snapped, "I demand to be put in instant communication with my uncle!"

She was universally ignored, even by young Richardson.

"We can detect him easy enough," Volos said. "But can we tell if it's him, rather than one of these Dawnworld craft? Although I suppose it's possible that they no longer use nuclear power."

Richardson turned and stared at him. "Has he talked you into believing that jetsam, sir?"

"I saw a starship at least a thousand times larger than anything in United Planets," his skipper told him without inflection. "Mr. Richardson, and you others, consider yourselves under the command of Citizens Bronston and Birdman. Countess Wyler, if that is your correct name, you attempted to confound me. Please keep in mind that I am captain of this vessel, no matter who your uncle may be. I expect the respect and cooperation of everyone aboard."

It was half an hour later before he spoke again.

And then it was to say, "On the face of it, below we have one of your Dawnworlds. It could be nothing else."

Below them was a world that was a park.

# XIII

It was as though you took a planet, approximately the size of Earth itself and transformed the whole into a landscaped garden. As though you made of the whole, a cinema set portraying the Garden of Eden, the Garden of Allah, the Promised Land, the Islands of the Blest, Zion, the Elysian Fields . . . what will you, for Paradise.

Rita Daniels hissed her breath in.

Takashi said shakily, "I can detect a nuclear powered ship. Only one. Seemingly larger than our own size."

Rita said, unthinking, "Uncle Max's yacht. It's the fastest . . ." Then she clammed up.

Ronny said, "Try to pinpoint it, Lieutenant." He looked at the captain. "No radio contact? No nothing?"

The captain shook his head. "I would think there would be some sort of patrol. Some sort of defense mechanism. But there doesn't seem to be. I can't even pick up any radio waves."

"Possibly they don't use radio waves any longer," Birdman muttered.

Richardson looked at him in disgust. "You've got to use radio waves," he said. "You can't run an advanced technology without radio waves."

Phil Birdman said, "You mean, you can't run *our* technology without radio waves."

Richardson blinked. "Just how far ahead of us are they supposed to be?"

Nobody answered him.

Ronny said to the captain, "What do you say we orbit her a few times, coming closer slowly?"

Several hours later, it was Rita who said, mystified, "But there aren't any cities."

And Phil Birdman said, disbelief in his own voice, "Maybe they don't use cities, either."

Takashi said, "There are a few worlds in United Planets that don't have cities."

"Yes," the captain muttered, "but the most backward of all. Places like Kropotkin, the anarchist experiment, and the planet Mother, with the Stone Age naturalists. By the looks of this world, the whole thing has been landscaped. That's not exactly within the capabilities of either anarchists or nature lovers, who refuse to utilize any inventions more complicated than the bow and arrow."

Ronny said thoughtfully, "Early man didn't have cities. They first came in as defense centers for the new developing agriculturalists, against rading nomads. Later on, they became centers for trade, and when social labor came in, large numbers of people had to live close together to work in manufacture."

"What are you getting at?" Rita asked.

"Well, perhaps these people, if they actually have matter converters, no longer need manufacturing or trade. No longer have to live in each others' laps."

The captain muttered, "I can't even make out individual houses. Or, for that matter, any sign of agriculture."

Mendlesohn said, awe in his voice, "Do you think that this could be a whole planet just devoted to being a park? Possibly their other planets are so built up and crowded that they've kept this one just for the sheer beauty of it."

Phil Birdman said, "Look at that herd of deer, or whatever they are!" His voice tuned low. "The Happy Hunting Ground."

"What?" Ronny asked.

"Nothing. How long does it take to breed out of a people, the instinct of the chase?"

Takashi said suddenly, "There. There's a city for you. And it's not too far from where I detected the nuclear powered spacecraft."

It was an area of possibly a square mile and the buildings were unique, even at a distance.

The captain looked at Ronny Bronston.

Ronny thought about it. "Let's drop closer," he said. "From all we know, if they'd wanted to crisp us they could have done so long before this. A race that could produce a spaceship as large as the one you saw, would have weapons to match."

They hovered over the complex of buildings, descending slowly, until the screens could pick out considerable detail.

"There in the center," Richardson said, "a pyramid. It looks like a Mayan pyramid."

"What is a Mayan pyramid?" Rita asked. Her voice held the same awe of this strange world as did the others.

Ronny said, "Your Earth history has been neglected, my dear. You spent too much of your time reading up on the strongmen. The Mayans were an early civilization in the southern part of North America. They . . ." He broke off suddenly as something came to him. "This isn't a city. It's a complex of religious buildings. Maybe schools, things like that, too. But it's not a city. Not in the sense of large numbers of persons living in it."

"There's one thing for sure"—Phil nodded—"there aren't

a good many people down there. What's that, on top of the pyramid?"

The skipper focused the small zoom-screen, quickly flashed if off again, his face pale.

"What's the matter, Captain?" Richardson asked. "Why didn't you throw it up on the large screen for the rest of us?"

Volos said to Ronny tightly. "Didn't you tell us that these so-called Dawnmen were sort of a copperish color?"

"That's right. Great, beautiful physical specimens. Rather a golden color."

The captain fiddled with his small zoomer again, finally located something and switched it to the compartment's large screen for all to see.

It was a small group of the Dawnworld people, both men and women. All were dressed in no more than loin cloths, or short kilts. All seemed approximately twenty-five years of age. All were in obvious sparkling health.

"These, eh?" the captain said, his voice strange.

Ronny looked at him. "Yes, of course. Those are the Dawnmen. They don't look particularly hostile or aggressive, do they?"

Volos said very slowly, "That wasn't a Dawnman on the top of the pyramid."

Ronny said, "If Baron Wyler is in the vicinity, it means two things: No matter how much of a headstart he got on us, he hasn't managed to get what he came after, as yet. Which means, in turn, that we've got to get a move on."

All the others looked at him.

"Well, what's the program?" Birdman asked.

"The Baron—if that's his craft we've detected—is on the ground," Ronny said thoughtfully. "We're going to have to land, too. Skipper, what say that you edge over a mile or so, beyond the limits of this city, or whatever it is, and drop one of us to reconnoiter?"

The captain turned to his control panel, silently.

He drifted the *Pisa* to the north, brought it down carefully in what was seemingly an isolated glen, devoid of life.

Ronny went to the hatch, Birdman and Takashi accompanying him, the others remaining in the control compartment, glued to the screens.

Lieutenant Takashi eyed the scanners built into the bulkhead over the hatch. "Almost identical to Earth atmosphere, Bronston," he reported.

Ronny said, "Well, here goes nothing, then."

The captain came up behind them.

"Citizen Birdman, Lieutenant, would you leave me with Citizen Bronston for a moment?"

Phil's eyebrows raised and he looked at Ronny, but then shrugged, and following the junior officer, went back into the control room.

Ronny asked, "What was it you saw at the top of the pyramid?"

"That's what I came back to tell you. I thought perhaps you'd just as well not alarm the girl—and the balance of the ship's complement, for that matter."

Ronny looked at him.

The captain cleared his throat. "It was what seemed to be an altar, and on it, a man."

"A Dawnman?"

"An Earthman. Or, to be more accurate, I suppose, a Phrygian. But, at any rate, a member of the human race, not a Dawnman."

Ronny sucked in air. Finally, he said, "All right. Drop me. Then take off again. I'll keep in touch, through

Agent Birdman. If anything happens to me, he's in command."

"Right," Volos said. There was a certain respect in his voice now, which had hardly been there in his early dealings with the Section G operatives.

When Ronny Bronston had gotten a good thousand yards from the *Pisa*, he turned and waved; and seconds later, it lifted off. He watched it fade away, upward and out.

He turned and looked about him.

It was still a park. A garden.

He shook his head in disbelief.

And not ten feet from him, some sort of door opened in empty space. For the briefest of moments, he could see into what seemed to be living quarters of a man-type being. Chairs, tables, decorations. . . .

But then a body blocked his view. A Dawnman came out and began walking toward him. The door, or whatever the opening was closed again.

Ronny was gaping, his jaw sagging. He shook his head for clarity.

The Dawnman, walking briskly and looking to neither left nor right, passed him by no more than three feet.

He could have stepped off a pedestal in a Greek temple devoted to the god Apollo. He was approximately six and a half feet tall and would have weighed approximately one hundred and ninety. His skin was golden, his hair dark cream. His eyes were blue and very clear, and there was the slightest of smiles on his lips.

He wasn't ignoring Ronny Bronston blindly, he was ignoring him enthusiastically, avidly, even vigorously, if that made sense.

He walked right on by and went about his business.

Ronny stood there for a long moment, blankly.

Perhaps the other was blind.

No. Ridiculous. A man didn't stride along as carefree as this young man was doing, without benefit of sight. He was about to top a slight hill, and would be lost to view. On an impulse, Ronny ran after him.

He called, "Say!"

The Dawnman either didn't hear, or didn't bother to answer. He strode on. Back from him floated a trill of song. Well, not exactly a song. Sort of a happy cross between song and whistle. It had a beautiful lilt.

Ronny called, realizing that the use of Earth Basic was ridiculous, "Wait! I want to talk to you!"

But the Dawnman passed over the rise and, by the time Ronny Bronston got to the top of the hillock, the Dawnman had disappeared.

Ronny looked about him, bewildered. There was no place for him to have gone in such short order. But then he remembered how the Dawnman had emerged from what had seemed open space. Without doubt, he had disappeared into another such . . . such . . . What was it?

And even with these thoughts in mind, Ronny walked full into . . . what was it? He smashed, at full pace, into an invisible barrier. He sat down, abruptly, his hand to his nose, which, he at first thought, must be broken. It wasn't. In a couple of minutes, still sitting, he got the nosebleed under control.

Then he stared accusingly at . . . at what? At nothing. Immediately before him seemed a beautifully kept lawn leading to a small grove of trees. Beyond the grove he could see a stream of unbelievably clear water.

He reached a hand forward, tentatively.

He could feel . . . what? A glass-like substance? He supposed so. He traced it from the ground up as far as he could reach, and then he walked slowly along it, ever feeling.

Seemingly, it was a wall. But he could see through it perfectly. No matter how close he brought his eyes, he could not see it, however.

He could hear his communicator hum in his pocket. He took it out and flicked open the lid. Phil Birdman was on the screen.

He said, anxiously, "For a minute, there, we thought we saw one of these Dawnmen right near you."

"You did."

"Well, what happened to him?"

Ronny said sourly, "He evidently came out of one house, walked down the street aways and into another."

Phil said, "Are you all right?"

"Except for a busted nose, I'm all right. This planet isn't depopulated. They evidently just don't like the idea of cluttering up the scenery with a lot of buildings, so they camouflage them. For all I know. I'm in the middle of a big city right now. No, I guess I couldn't be, or I'd see more people out here in the open."

"Camouflage? We don't see any camouflage."

"Oh, knock it," Ronny told him. "It's *perfect* camouflage, of course, you can't see it. Have you got in touch with Earth?"

"Right. I talked with Sid Jakes. He said to play it by ear."

Ronny grunted. "Tell him I'm playing it by nose, instead." He flicked the communicator off.

With no other idea of what to do in mind, he walked the direction of the city, or religious buildings, or whatever they were.

He rounded a bend and came upon what could only

be a picnic. A group of the Dawnpeople, about ten of them, were seated on the bank of a stream. There were both men and women, all seemingly somewhere between the ages of twenty and thirty: All absolutely perfect physical specimens. If anything, the perfection was its own drawback. They were, Bronston decided, too perfect.

Not a woman nor a man among them that wouldn't have met the highest standards of Tri-Di sex symbol back on Earth, or any of the other planets that continued the fan system of theater. No Greek goddess could have rivaled a single of these women in pulchritude. Paris would have had his work cut out, choosing whom to give his apple.

Ronny hesitated. Obviously, these people were at their leisure, enjoying themselves. He disliked to intrude.

But then it came to him, that given fusion power and matter converters, they must have considerable in the way of leisure. Besides, they would be interested in him as a complete alien. He might as well take the plunge.

He stepped nearer and said, "I beg your pardon," feeling like a flat at the words, but the ice had to be broken somehow. He assumed that a race this advanced would have some method of communicating with him. Some technician who . . .

But then, Baron Wyler's words came back to him: *these Dawnpeople are not intelligent.*

Nonsense! On the face of it . . .

But on the face of it, they didn't even see him.

He stepped closer.

They went on with their picnic, if that's what it was. They ignored him, completely, enthusiastically. He stepped so close that they couldn't possibly have missed his presence.

And it wasn't as though they were blind. He could see them performing actions that obviously required the coordination of hand and eye.

One of them, an absolutely perfectly formed girl wearing nothing but sandals and a colorful kilt, picked up a handful of sand and gravel from the stream's bank and turned with it to a low table. There was, on the table, a device that reminded Ronny of nothing so much as a primitive coffee grinder he had once seen in an Earth museum. She poured the dirt into a funnel-shaped hole on the top and touched a switch or stud.

She opened a small door and brought forth what was seemingly a piece of fruit, though unrecognizable as to type by the Section G agent. She began to munch it.

Ronny Bronston closed his eyes in surrender.

He said, in sudden exasperation, "Look, won't somebody give me a steer?"

They still didn't notice him.

He looked at the gathering more closely. There were several of the coffee-grinder devices. Evidently, they were in continual use. Some of the Dawnpeople were drinking from intricately shaped glasses, some eating various unidentifiable foodstuffs. They laughed. One or two sang, from time to time, in that strange trilling manner Ronny had heard earlier from his first contact.

They were obviously having one whale of a time.

He stared at the devices.

With unbelievably good luck, he had stumbled, within a half hour of the first landing on the Dawnworld, on one of their matter converters. They were paying no attention to him. He might as well have not existed. Suppose he took one of the things up. What would they do? It was hard to believe that any of these people were apt to re-

sort to violence. And most certainly they carried no weapons.

But that gave him pause. Given the occasion, who
could say but that they were capable of pouring a handful of sand into one of their gismos and bring forth a
pistol to end all pistols?"

But this was his obvious chance. For whatever reason,
the Baron was evidently still on this planet. His expedition, thus far, had failed. If Ronny could acquire one of
these working models of matter transformers, Section G's
technicians could possibly take it apart, duplicate it,
come up with larger models.

He went so far as to tentatively reach forth a hand toward the nearest. They continued to ignore him. By not a
flicker of eye did they admit to his presence.

Ronny drew his hand back.

He wondered wildly if he were invisible to them. But
no. Obviously these people were human. Perhaps not
exactly of his genus, but most certainly they were of the
species *Homo*. This world of theirs had obviously been
landscaped to please their own taste. It pleased his as
well. They saw what he saw.

He stared at the matter converter. There it was. There
was victory over the Baron and his plans to dominate.

Something kept him. Intuition? What? He didn't know.
He was disgusted with himself. Why not snatch it up?

His communicator hummed. Impatiently, he snatched
it from his pocket. It was Birdman again.

"What is it?" Ronny snapped.

"Baron Wyler," the Indian said urgently. "He's made
contact with us."

"Oh." Ronny paused. The Baron's space yacht was considerably larger than the four man United Planets Space

Cruiser. Ronny had no doubt that it was armed with the most efficient weapons the Baron could find.

He asked, "What does he want?"

"Help."

## XIV

For the moment, he didn't allow himself to dwell further on that. He snapped, "Tell the skipper to get down here and pick me up."

"Right," Phil said, and faded.

Ronny Bronston went back to the grove in which the *Pisa* had set him down such a short time before. His mind was in a whirl. He held in abeyance Birdman's information about the Baron, and tried to find some rhyme or reason about his own discoveries.

Wyler and Fitzjames must have been right. These people were not intelligent in the sense of the word that *Homo sapiens* implied. *Intelligent, somehow,* he supposed. *But with a different intelligence.* He shook his head in exasperation.

The *Pisa* came gently to rest, and he went over to it as quickly as was safe.

The captain and Birdman were at the lock when he entered.

Ronny snapped, "What's all this . . .?"

Phil Birdman said, "Wyler took the initiative. I suppose he picked us up as quickly as we did his yacht. At any rate, he contacted us. He says he wants help."

"Help from what?"

"He didn't say."

They went back to the control room and joined the others.

Ronny said, "It's a trap, he's trying to suck us in."

Captain Volos shook his head. "I don't think so. On

the screen, he looked like a broken man. Obviously, he knows you'll place him under arrest. That all his plans are shot."

Phil Birdman said, "Listen, let's leave him in whatever juice he's stewing in. If it's a trap, we won't spring it. If he's really in trouble, it couldn't happen to a nicer guy."

Rita held a small fist to her mouth.

Ronny shook his head. "No," he said. "Let's get over there. No matter what, he's our people, and we're all in a strange land." He grumbled, "A damnably strange land."

While the captain and his crew turned to their ship's controls, Rita looked at Ronny Bronston. She said softly, "You're not the worst person around, young fella."

Ronny chuckled wryly. "The term is *old man*, not young fella." He turned to the others and gave them a quick rundown on his meagre adventures.

He earned their disbelieving stares.

Phil Birdman blurted, "Why didn't you slap one of them across the chops? That would have got a rise."

Ronny looked at him. "I didn't think of that." He paused. Then, "You wouldn't have, either. Somehow, there's a no-touch feeling in the air."

"Why didn't you put the lift on one of the converters, or whatever they are?"

Ronny scowled, "I don't know. The no-touch atmosphere entered into that, too."

Takashi said, "There is the Phrygian ship."

They brought it into the large screen.

"No sign of a fight, or anything," Phil Birdman said.

The space yacht was at rest in a lovely dell.

Volos looked at the Section G operatives.

Ronny took a breath and said, "All right. Set down next to them." He looked at the *Pisa's* three junior officers, finally deciding on Richardson. He said, "If I give you a gun, do you think you can keep from shooting me with it?"

The young ensign was embarrassed. "Yes, sir. Sorry about our earlier difficulties, sir."

Ronny said, "Richardson and I will go over and case the situation. I'll keep my communicator on, and in constant touch. Anything goes wrong, you take off. Birdman will be in charge. Does Wyler know that Citizeness Daniels is aboard?"

"I talked with Uncle Max," she said worriedly. "Can't I go with you?"

"Not yet," he said apologetically. "I'm afraid you're still a hostage. I doubt if he'll attack the *Pisa* as long as you're aboard."

Rita shook her head. "He wouldn't attack it, anyway. Something terrible has happened."

"We'll see," Ronny said. "Come on, Ensign."

Takashi saw them through the lock, and closed it behind. They crossed the seemingly neatly trimmed grass to the other craft. Ronny looked it over. A luxurious, highly powered yacht, probably as fast as anything UP could produce. And, obviously, well-armed to boot.

He had expected to be met by well disciplined, nattily uniformed spacemen of the Phrygian space forces, but instead, Count Fitzjames was the only one at the lock to greet them.

Ronny made a brief introduction, not hiding the fact that he was holding his communicator up. His right hand was ready for a quick draw.

Count Fitzjames said, the usual worry in his voice, "The Supreme Commandant is in his lounge. This way."

Baron Wyler was indeed in the lounge. He was sprawled, as though exhausted, in a deep chair. His eyes were wide and unseeing, and there was despair in his face.

Ronny stood before him and he looked up.

There was no more of the hail-fellow-well-met tone of voice. No friendly projection of personality, no all-embracing charm of the born leader of men.

Ronny and Ensign Richardson had seen no others on their way through the ship. It came to Ronny that whatever had happened, this was no trap. Neither Wyler nor Fitzjames were shamming. Somehow, their expedition had become a cropper.

"All right," Ronny said. "What happened? What did you mean when you radioed us for help?"

The Baron said wearily, "I can't navigate this craft, nor can the Count. We have no way of getting back."

Ronny stared at him. "Where's your crew?"

"They've evidently been sacrificed to the gods—or something along that line. Cutting the heart out with what looked like an obsidian knife!" a spasm of horror went over the former strongman's face.

The Baron didn't seem to be particularly coherent. Ronny sat himself down and looked at the scholarly Count. "Suppose you bring me up to date."

"I am not sure I can, in complete detail; but I have a theory."

"All right, take your time. Richardson, take a look through the ship."

Richardson left.

The Count said unhappily, "I am not quite sure where to start." He looked into Ronny's face. "Citizen Bronston, has it ever occurred to you that perhaps primitive man, say Cro-Magnon man, might have been more intelligent than modern man?" He hurried on before getting an answer. "Don't confuse intelligence with accumulated

145

knowledge. You can take a man with an I.Q. of ninety and fill him with a great deal of accumulated knowledge. Keep at it long enough and you can get him a doctor's degree. On the other hand, you can take a man with an I.Q. of 150 and place him in the right—or rather, the wrong—surroundings and he'll wind up with very little education at all. He'll be smart, but will possess little accumulated knowledge.

"In primitive times, if a man was slow in the head, he died. The race needed better brains and bred for them. But as we solved the problems of defense against other animals and against nature, and we learned to feed, clothe and shelter ourselves, the need became less pressing. Our less intelligent survived, and lived to breed. Finally we achieve to the point where there was an abundance of everything for all, and the need of having superior brains fell away. No longer were the most brainy in the community given the best food, the best women—the best the community could offer in all desirable things. They were no longer at a premium."

"What in Zen are you driving at?" Ronny asked impatiently.

"One of my theories is that these Dawnmen are the end product of having an abundance for all for a megayear or so. They don't *need* intelligence."

Ronny took a breath. "All right, and what are some more of your theories?" Through this, the Baron was sitting, staring into emptiness again.

Fitzjames said, "If I am correct, in the Dawnworld culture, the form of their early industrial revolution differed from ours on Earth. Remember my using the example of the caste system in India? Well, on the first Dawnworld, wherever it was, automation didn't finally take over, conformity did. What it became was a very high industrial level, beehive-type culture. The individual workers are genetically predisposed to particular kinds of endeavor, and very readily and rapidly learn that specialty . . . but can't learn anything else.

"They're a contented people, a happy people. Everybody is happy—or he's a genetic defective, and disposed of. Because he *is* a genetic defective, or he'd be happy."

Ronny was staring at him. The scholar cleared his throat and went on. "They are evidently not aggressive or warlike. But they're insect-like in the all-out-and-no-counting-the-casualties defense of their territories and their ways of doing things. They probably can't be aggressive, because they're one hundred percent ritualistic, and they have no ritual for aggression, nor for exploiting a new planet. Their expanding to new planets probably ended megayears ago.

"We were at first amazed, when we landed, that they ignored our presence. But they couldn't do anything else, because they don't have any rituals that acknowledge our existence. They haven't any rituals that take strangers, whatever their business, into account at all."

The Baron looked up. He sighed deeply and said, "Tell him, Fitzjames. I grow weary of your pedantic talk."

The count hurried on. "They do have rituals that concern treatment of criminals. Steal something from them, and you come under those rituals and your classification as *stranger*—to be ignored—is superceded by the new classification *criminal,* and that, they do react to."

"Tell him," the Baron said petulantly.

"Their defectives are killed in a human sacrifice ceremony, which must have religious aspects going back to the very dawn of their culture."

Ronny looked from one of them to the other. "You sent

out your men to grab any of their devices not nailed down."

"Yes," the Baron said.

The count continued. "My theory is that the little aliens, whose planets were destroyed by changing their atmospheres, did much the same. They took a longer time. They charted a considerable number of the star systems the Dawnmen occupy. They photographed. They operated very slowly, evidently fascinated. But then they took their steps and tried to appropriate some of the devices these Dawnmen use. Perhaps they tried to trade for them, buy them, loan them, or whatever, but there was no possible way to do so. The Dawnmen are simply not interested in any contact whatsoever with any alien race. So the little aliens finally resorted to theft—and that was their end."

Richardson came back into the lounge. He said to Ronny, "There's nobody else aboard."

The Baron said, "We watched it all, the Count and I. The men were taken one by one to the top of the pyramid. It was an elaborate ceremony. It must go back to a period when they were on the level of the Aztecs. They cut open the chest cavity and pulled the still throbbing heart out. The Count and I watched from an altitude of about one hundred feet. There was nothing we could do. It was obvious to us that if we attempted to use weapons, they would have destroyed us in split seconds."

"Had we interfered," the count said, "we, too, would have become criminals. As it was, we were the only ones who had not attempted theft, and hence were left alone."

The Baron ended the story. "I can operate this craft well enough to take off and land, but I am no navigator. I request that one or two of your officers be sent to help us."

Ronny opened his mouth to answer, but, at that moment, a new element entered into the lounge of the spacecraft.

From nowhere a voice came into the consciousness of each of them.

*You are at last correct, Maximilian Wyler. You must return to the planet which our researching of your mind tells us you think of as Mother Earth. There is naught for you here.*

*Ronald Bronston, we detect that your motives for landing upon this . . . Dawnworld . . . were not criminal in intent, nor have you committed depredation upon us. It is our custom to send warning to stranger worlds —who are potential depredators—by the way of strangers who have landed among us, but have committed no criminal act. You are such. However, our researching your health indicated that your life span has been so altered that perhaps it would not encompass the period required to spread the warning. Hence, we have made certain rectifications so that your span of years will equal that of a normal lifetime as we know it to be—some two and a half of what you call centuries.*

Ronny Bronston sucked in air.

"Who are you?" Count Fitzjames blurted.

*Researching your own mind, Felix Fitzjames, brings to our attention that in attempting to analyze our culture, you compared our society to the caste system of your India. Indeed you had elements of correctness. But why did you forget about the Brahmins amond us? Why did you assume that the equivalents of the sudras with whom you have come in contact, were the sum total of our race?*

The voice addressed them as a group again.

*Go back to your Mother Earth. Do not be afraid of the Dawnworlds. Felix Fitzjames was correct to this extent: We are not aggressive. We have no designs against you. So long as you have none against us, our cultures need never conflict. Farewell. . . .*

"Wait!" Baron Wyler cried out. "Why should I go back to Mother Earth? Why not to my own planet, Phrygia?"

*You would find it difficult to breath, Maximilian Wyler. When our people are interfered with, they trace back to the planet from which the criminal element came so as to preserve themselves from additional predators in the future. The atmosphere of Phrygia is now composed of methane, ammonia and hydrogen. To the extent that Ronald Bronston succeeds in his mission of warning, a like fate will be saved your other worlds. And now we will communicate with you no longer. Farewell. . . .*

And suddenly there was an emptiness in the space yacht's lounge.

At long last, Ronny Bronston looked at the aging Count Fitzjames. "Are you still so sure they aren't intelligent?" he asked wryly. "At least on the highest level, we can expect cooperation. Where there's logical intelligence, you can communicate."

But Felix Fitzjames, his lips pale, was shaking his head. "Is a Brahmin less castebound than the lower castes? Does a queen bee have any more freedom of will than a worker?"

Ronny, and, to a lesser degree, Baron Wyler, were scowling at him.

The aged scholar was still shaking his head. "Perhaps the voice we just heard came from those who think of themselves as intelligent; but if it's gone through two megayears of this culture, it must live by pure ritual, too. Because its rituals are somewhat different and more complex than the lower castes', it possibly believes it isn't a pre-programmed mechanism."

"I'm not sure I get what you're driving at," Ronny muttered.

Fitzjames was feeling it out, even as he talked. "One of the early problems of the cybernetic researchers was the fact that—to be intelligent, an entity must be capable of inconsistent behavior. But that means not to be logically predictable. This brings the frustration that an intelligent-inconsistent machine—which would be capable of exercising judgment—cannot be reliable in the sense of predictable. That is, the closer they come to a truly intelligent cybernetic device, the more it approaches the unreliable performance of a living organism."

The Baron shifted in his chair, as though not following. He had remained silent, in shock, since the revelation of the end of his ambition, his dream . . . his very world.

Fitzjames turned his full attention to Ronny. "Ants are very reliable living organisms, an entymologist can predict exactly what a particular ant of a particular type will do. It's genetically pre-programmed. The voice we just heard is a part also of a genetically pre-programmed system; it must be just as reliable and, therefore, invariable as the lower castes. An anthill, termitarium, or beehive is a true totalitarian state—and in a true totalitarian state, the Führer, Dictator, Caesar, or whatever, is just as much controlled by the rituals and taboos as every other member of the state. This Dawnworld culture would not have been stable for such a period, if its Brahmins had not been just as rigidly unintelligent as every other entity in the system."

He shook his head once again, an element of despair

in the movement. "I am afraid we can look for no hope of eventual understanding between our cultures to these supposed intelligent elements in the Dawnworlds."

The two Section G agents, Rita Daniels, and Lieutenant Takashi moved from the *Pisa* to the Baron Wyler's space yacht for the trip in return to United Planets.

For the first few days there was little communication between them. No desire for words. There was a pervading atmosphere of mental lassitude, ennui.

It was toward the end of this period that Ronny Bronston found himself alone in the lounge with Rita Daniels. They had not been avoiding each other, it was just that they had failed to contact.

He brought her a drink from the bar and one for himself.

"What are you going to do?" he asked.

She looked at him thoughtfully. "I suppose I'll stick with Uncle Max. He . . . he needs someone now."

"The last member of the team, eh?"

She looked to see if there was bitterness in his face, but it was neutral.

"I suppose so," she said. "I believe Count Fitzjames plans to offer his services to the Octagon. After all, he is the nearest thing to an authority we have on the Dawnworlds."

Ronny said, "Don't worry about your uncle. The Wylers in life make out all right. Through his power hunger, in one fell swoop, he was the cause of the deaths of more people than Ghengis Kahn, Tamerlane, Stalin and Hitler all rolled into an unhappy one. But he'll make out."

She said lowly, "You hate my uncle, don't you?"

He shook his head at her. "I don't hate anyone. I'm rapidly coming to the conclusion that the more you learn about the workings of individuals, cultures and even the ultimate destiny of the species, the less possible is it to hate anybody. As I recall, you were particularly interested in the ultimate destiny of the race."

"I *was*," she said wryly. "Now, I'm not so sure about it."

# AFTERMATH

After all reports were through, Ronny Bronston came to his feet and reached in his pocket for his wallet. He tossed it to the desk of Ross Metaxa.

"My badge," he said.

Metaxa and Sid Jakes looked at him.

The Commissioner of Section G said, "What are you going to do?"

"First, I'm going to ask a girl I've met recently to marry me. Then I'm going to migrate to Shangri-La. You can turn over to United Planets the job of spreading the warning against bothering the Dawnworlds."

Sid Jakes chuckled. "Shangri-La? What's there, my disillusioned friend?"

"The hedonistic ethic."

"Eat, drink and be merry, for tomorrow we die, eh?"

"Something like that."

"Great," Metaxa growled. "But it's hardly a teaching to be followed by a whole species."

"Oh," Ronny said. "Why not? But what I do know is that the purpose of Section G is gone. The pressing need to hurry man toward his final destiny no longer appeals to me. I have seen his final destiny, and it has little appeal."

Ross Metaxa, moist of eye as always as though from too little sleep or too much alcohol, looked at him wearily. "You haven't thought this Dawnworld threat through to its conclusion, Ronny."

His resigning agent grunted amusement. "There is no threat. We leave them alone, they leave us alone."

The Section G head grunted contempt of that opinion.

"Do you know the legal doctrine of the *attractive nuisance?* Swimming pools are classified as 'attractive nuisances,' for instance. It's a legal doctrine based on the proposition that something like a swimming pool is a natural, inevitable attraction to small children—children, who simply aren't old enough to be competent to take care of themselves; and who aren't old enough, either, to be wise enough to realize they can't. Children simply can't be fenced in at all times, so they can't wander into neighborhood swimming pools and drown. So the 'attractive nuisance' laws make the owner of the swimming pool liable, which forces the pool owner to put a fence around the pool, instead of saying—all the children in the neighborhood should have fences built around them.

"As I recall, the classic case that started that legislation rolling was a company, in the old days, that had a beautiful 75 x 125 foot concrete-lined pool on company property. One weekend, when operations were shut down, some kids sneaked onto the company land and dove in. The first two were in before they discovered that it was the company's sulfuric acid storage vat."

Ronny was getting the point.

Metaxa said, "More than one of the member planets of United Planets are in the 'children' category. Some of them will have populations with hysterical reactions to the existence of our passive-but-appallingly-deadly-threat Dawnworlds. They'll want to provoke war. Then there'll be, inevitably, the crooks who want to steal some of those magnificent gadgets, that magnificent science. Baron Wyler was an example. There'll probably even be religious cranks, who'll want to send missionaries."

Ronny said, "So we still need a Section G, to act as a

fence around this 'attractive nuisance.' Is that your point?"

Ross Metaxa growled, "You once asked me if you'd been conned into joining Section G. The answer was 'yes.' It also would have been 'yes,' if you'd asked the question about Sid, here—or, about myself, for that matter. The job's to be done, we have to take what measures we must to do it. The question is asked, 'am I my brother's keeper?'" He looked deeply into the other's eyes. "The answer, Ronny, is 'yes.'"

Sid Jakes chuckled. "Meaning, of course, that a keeper is one who cares for and controls the actions of one who is incompetent, irresponsible or insane."

Ronny looked at Sid Jakes. "I know of a girl you ought to get busy on, recruiting into Section G. She'll make a top agent." He slowly reached down to take up the wallet, which contained his badge.

But Metaxa anticipated him, picked it up and dropped it into a desk drawer.

Ronny looked at him.

Metaxa brought forth another wallet and tossed it over. The badge inside gleamed gold at Ronny's touch.

Ross Metaxa growled, "Recruit this girl yourself, Bronston. If necessary, using whatever dirty tricks are required to rope her into our service. That's one of the prime duties of operatives of supervisor rank."

www.ingramcontent.com/pod-product-compliance
Lightning Source LLC
Chambersburg PA
CBHW020648180626
46816CB00003B/1174